MAITLAND'S REPLY

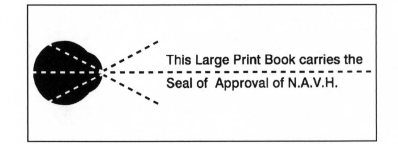

This Large Print Book carries the
Seal of Approval of N.A.V.H.

MAITLAND'S REPLY

JAMES PATRICK HUNT

THORNDIKE PRESS
A part of Gale, Cengage Learning

GALE
CENGAGE Learning™

Detroit • New York • San Francisco • New Haven, Conn • Waterville, Maine • London

GALE
CENGAGE Learning™

Copyright © 2009 by James Patrick Hunt.
Thorndike Press, a part of Gale, Cengage Learning.

Thorndike Press® Large Print Core.
The text of this Large Print edition is unabridged.
Other aspects of the book may vary from the original edition.
Set in 16 pt. Plantin.
Printed on permanent paper.

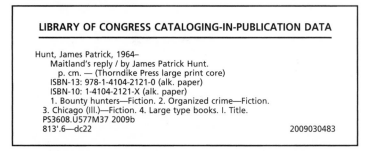

LIBRARY OF CONGRESS CATALOGING-IN-PUBLICATION DATA

Hunt, James Patrick, 1964–
    Maitland's reply / by James Patrick Hunt.
        p. cm. — (Thorndike Press large print core)
    ISBN-13: 978-1-4104-2121-0 (alk. paper)
    ISBN-10: 1-4104-2121-X (alk. paper)
    1. Bounty hunters—Fiction. 2. Organized crime—Fiction.
3. Chicago (Ill.)—Fiction. 4. Large type books. I. Title.
    PS3608.U577M37 2009b
    813'.6—dc22   2009030483

Published in 2009 by arrangement with Tekno Books and Ed Gorman.

"To get rich is glorious."

— Deng Xiaoping

ONE

There was an old-style metal rotating fan that sat on a battered green filing cabinet. It would turn to the left of its base, stop when it reached the extent of its arc, pause, and then go back to its right. Turning slowly, stopping, repeating, measuring out a beat for a long, hot afternoon.

Step back from the fan and turn around. Three men in the room. The room being a barbershop. One of the men was wearing a yellow smock. With short snips, he worked at the hair of another man sitting in the barber's chair. A third man sat on a red chair that had steel arms with rust freckles on them. The man on the red chair did not read the magazines on the chair next to his. He smoked his cigarette and sat quietly. He wore a blue For Members Only jacket despite the still, damp heat of the day. His name was Tommy Kui, and this was his place.

A small barbershop in the Chinatown section of New York. Tucked away and unnoticeable to the *gwai lo,* the whites. There are plenty like it in Chinatown. Small barbershops with dated furnishings and lace in the windows. From outside it seems humble and unassuming. The sign in the window says the haircuts are seven dollars. The massage parlor is at the back. At Tommy Kui's, there were usually two girls on duty. They would give you mooncakes and tea before your massage and more if you had the money. Hundred bucks for the handwork, three hundred for the works, tip not included.

A stranger could know that or not know that from seeing the front of the shop. But if the stranger was wise, if he possessed that sixth sense that said *trouble,* he would know there was something of the night about Tommy Kui and his man behind the barber's chair. Something menacing and dangerous. If they wanted a Chinese girl bad enough, they would dismiss that fear and stick around. It could be worth it. Or they could stick around for a seven-dollar cut.

The man in the barber chair wanted both the haircut and the handwork. He was an old Chinese, between sixty and seventy, and he was in no hurry. And it took him a moment or two to register it when another man came in the front door.

A man in his thirties, tall for a Chinese, wearing gray slacks and a black suit jacket and a white shirt. Put a tie on him and he could pass for a Wall Street trader or businessman. But his eyes were alert and aware. His name was Frank Chang.

He stopped in the middle of the shop and for a moment nobody said anything.

Jimmy Kui drew on his cigarette, taking his time before he exhaled. He looked at Chang for a moment before dipping his head into a nod.

Frank Chang said, "I need a cut," speaking Chinese-Cantonese when he said it.

Jimmy Kui regarded him for a few moments more. Then he nodded to the barber behind the chair.

The barber tapped the old customer on the shoulder. They spoke in Cantonese to each other, the old man protesting that he wanted to get his massage, goddammit, the barber shaking his head and saying, no, come back later. A minute later, the old man was gone and Frank took a seat in the barber's chair.

The barber put the white cover around Chang's shoulders and tied it behind his neck. He said to Chang, "How about a shave?"

Frank Chang was looking at Kui when he answered. "Sure," he said.

The barber dampened Chang's face with the hot towel and then put the lather on. After that, he opened a drawer to get the straight razor. It was underneath a meat cleaver. The barber sharpened the blade on a leather strop and then came and stood at Frank Chang's side to cut the first swath.

The blade was approximately an inch from Chang's face when the barber heard it.

Not a click, but a double click. And there's a difference. In the span of a career, a criminal gets to know guns. If not by sound, then by feel.

The blade was hovering inches away from Frank Chang's cheek, just a drop away from the jugular vein in his neck. But the barber pulled the blade back and let his eyes drop to the sound of the double click.

And there it was. The long barrel of a .357 revolver pointing up at his genitals.

Frank Chang was still looking at Kui when he spoke.

Chang said, "Go ahead."

Carefully, slowly, the barber started to shave Frank Chang.

From where he was sitting, Jimmy Kui could not see the gun. It was hidden beneath the white cover. But he was aware that something had changed in the barber's demeanor . . . fear and respect replacing blood lust. At least for now. Jimmy Kui was starting to recognize Frank Chang, too. A Red Pole from the White Lotus Triad. An enforcer.

Kui said, "What do you want?"

Frank Chang said, "You've made offense."

"To who?"

"The White Lotus."

"Ah," Kui said. "You own Chinatown now?"

Chang responded with a thin smile. It was all it was worth. He said, "Chu-mei's."

"What about it?"

"Your gang's been putting the squeeze on him. Two hundred a week."

"Is that what he said?"

"That's what it is," Chang said.

Jimmy Kui shrugged and smiled and drew on his cigarette. He said, "Chu-mei can afford that. We make sure his restaurant is protected."

"It's already being protected. By us."

And had been for almost ten years. All restaurants in Chinatown received protection from one triad or another. But only one. Jimmy Kui knew this. Yet it hadn't stopped him from sending three of his men to Chu-mei's and asking Chu-mei for a weekly protection fee. Chu-mei, under the protection of the White Lotus Triad, politely refused. Kui's men smiled and left and returned the next week and broke some things. A table and a few glasses and a waiter were shoved to the ground. Nothing too serious, but a message was sent that payment would have to be made or it would get a lot rougher. Another Chinese business-man threatened by Chinese gangsters, but this one was already supposed to be pro-tected. It shouldn't have to pay protection money to Kui's *liang jies* as well.

Jimmy Kui knew all this going in. But his goal was not so much to intimidate Chu-mei as it was to make the White Lotus lose face. If he could get away with it at Chu-mei's, any other turf protected by the White Lotus would be fair game. Easy game.

Frank Chang had been sent to attempt to mediate this dispute. If it could be resolved peacefully, good. If not . . .

Frank Chang said, "Perhaps you didn't know."

He was giving Kui a chance now. An op-portunity to say that he didn't know, that he didn't know that Chu-mei was protected by the White Lotus. He didn't know and he had been mistaken and to please convey his regrets to the White Lotus *shu chan* and to Chu-mei as well for the misunderstanding. But Kui wasn't interested. Perhaps because Frank had come alone. Perhaps because he thought the White Lotus was past its prime and that it was time for a new guard to take over. Perhaps because he smoked too much opium and it had fogged his better judgment over the years.

Kui said, "I knew." He gestured with his head to another man on his left, Frank's right, standing in the doorway. Frank Chang moved as he saw the third man raise his sawed-off shotgun to kill him, Frank grabbing the sleeve of the barber and pulling him forward as he twisted the barber's chair. The barber took the shotgun blast in his back as Frank Chang dropped to the floor behind the chair, the third man racking the slide on the shotgun to give another blast. That was when Frank pointed the .357 revolver and shot him twice in the chest. Then Kui had his own pistol out and was shooting at the chair, but Frank was underneath it, pointing it up and steady as he pulled the trigger and shot Kui three times.

Three men were dead now as Frank Chang got to his feet and surveyed the damage. He wiped the shaving cream off his face and was looking in the mirror when he saw one of Kui's girls peeking around the corner. Her frightened expression seeing his eyes in the glass.

Frank said to the mirror, "Go back," with a firm voice that a parent would use to speak to a kid who was supposed to be upstairs and in bed. The girl vanished.

Frank Chang had been in this business long enough to know that the girl would not call the police and attempt to describe him or reveal what he had done. Like most of her kind, she probably didn't speak English. And even if she did, she wouldn't even consider bringing the American police into her world. This was Chinatown.

Two

Chinatown in Manhattan occupies a rectangle of approximately one by two miles. In that rectangle live around 300,000 Chinese. It is technically under the jurisdiction of the New York Police Department, but it operates more or less under its own laws. Many of its occupants, if not most, do not speak English and the Chinese are not quick to trust the police in any event. It is a culture that has reason to be skeptical of government authority, China having been ruled by gangsters and Communists for the last hundred years. There had been no democratic institutions before that and they would be slow to come in the future.

Frank Chang was not given to deep introspection on such matters. He did not think in terms of politics or history. Nor did he struggle with his identity or ask whether he was a Chinese first or an American second. He was a Red Pole in the White Lotus Triad, a sort of noncommissioned officer in that organization, and he thought in terms of the next job and comfort and, most importantly, survival. His role was that of enforcer, taskmaster. He had killed three men in a barbershop, two of them with a loud weapon, but he knew Chinatown well enough not to run once he left the barbershop. No one would call the police. Heads would be kept down, shots would be ignored, life and commerce would continue. Frank walked out and merged into the late afternoon mass of people and after walking the space of a block, he relaxed.

The men inside the barbershop had been fools. Greedy and stupid. They could have worked something out and still kept face, but they got cocky. Arrogant. They had chosen their deaths as they had chosen their lives.

Frank Chang walked through the neighborhood he had lived in for most of his life. Bustle and commerce and noise. Street vendors selling imitation perfumes, watches, and handbags. A couple of cooks in white uniforms and red hats having a break in the street, smoking cigarettes. Teenagers playing with their handheld video games.

It took Frank about twenty minutes to walk to Chol Soo's restaurant.

The host was wearing a threadbare suit and he gave a slight bow to Frank when he came in. Respect for Frank's rank as well as the man. Frank returned the gesture and said, "Is Chol Soo here?"

"In the kitchen," the host said.

Chol Soo was a noted chef, his dishes the envy of some of the best cooks in Taipei. He was also a Straw Sandal, the *chou hai*. A liaison officer in the White Lotus. His rank, such as it was, was on the same level as Chang's. But it was Chol Soo who would report to the *fu shan chu,* the Deputy Mountain Master, or the *shan chu* himself if the occasion so required. Like many officers in the triad, Chol Soo kept more than one home. An apartment in the Confucius Plaza in Manhattan and a home in Flushing, Queens. To the outside observer, this may not seem like much. But in Chinatown, it was a king's existence. Most Chinese there shared one-room tenements with five or six other family members and shared a bathroom with all the other families on the floor. Long hours, hard work, and then home to cramped quarters. This life was relieved by drug use, whores, and neverending gambling.

Chol Soo was assisting one of his cooks with a shark soup when Frank came into

17

the kitchen. Chol Soo was dressed like the other cooks in a white apron and hat, but his demeanor was different from theirs and their body language was deferential. Chol Soo acknowledged Frank and together they walked back to a small office.

Chol Soo said, "Would you like some tea?"

"No," Frank said. "It's too hot."

Chol Soo smiled. "You've been in America too long. We're not supposed to care if it's too hot for tea. Some water then?"

"Please."

Chol Soo got a bottle of water out of a small refrigerator behind his desk and handed it to Chang.

Chol Soo said, "Well?"

Frank Chang shook his head. "He didn't want to negotiate."

"Ah. So he's . . ."

"Yes. And two of his men." Frank shrugged. "It was what I expected."

Chol Soo said, "He should have known better." A sigh. "Well, Tsu will not be surprised."

Tsu "Walter" Fong was the *shan chu.* The Mountain Master. The Boss.

Chol Soo said, "Do you want a woman?"

It was a common question. After a Red Pole carried out an assassination, he usually wanted a woman or he wanted to gamble.

18

Or he wanted opium. Frank Chang avoided drugs and gambling had never held much allure for him. He liked women, though.

"Not now," he said. He had his own woman. A lady in Brooklyn whose husband was in Beijing for months at a time. It was a private thing, though, and he didn't want to discuss it with Chol Soo. Still, he didn't want to insult him either. So he said "not now" as opposed to refusing the offer.

Frank noticed that the man was hesitating, maybe to make a specific recommendation for a prostitute. Trying to fill up time and dead space.

Frank Chang said, "Is there something else?"

Chol Soo said, "Yes. I know it's soon, but Fong wants you to take another job. He wants you to leave tonight, in fact."

"What is it?"

Chol Soo said, "You know the Wu-Chai?"

The Wu-Chai Triad, based in San Francisco. "Yes," Frank said.

"You know they've branched out to Chicago?"

"I've heard."

"Fong has been negotiating with them."

"To keep them out of New York?"

"Partly, yes. But that's not the whole of it. He's offered to let them use you for a job in

Chicago."

And this Frank Chang understood. A "job" meant an assassination. The triads liked to bring people in from out of town. Get the killing done and be out of town that day. He'd done it before.

Chol Soo said, "He wants you to do this, but you can reject it if you please. The Wu-Chai will pay you though."

"How much?"

"Fifty. After it's done."

"Directly?"

"Yes."

"Fong is okay with this?"

"Yes."

Out of respect, though, Frank would have to kick something back to Fong. Five thousand should cover it. Not that Fong needed the money. The proceeds from his gambling houses and brothels and pirated DVDs brought him about seventy thousand dollars a week. But he would want tribute from Chang as a sign of respect. Both Chol Soo and Chang understood this.

Frank said, "Do you know anything more about it?"

"No," Chol Soo said. "Nor does Fong. You fly out tonight. When you get there, you take your orders from their deputy *shan chu*. Do you know him?"

"No."

"His name is Wong Ming-Hai. His American name is Preston Wong. He is a businessman, ostensibly. A clean-looking sophisticate. But don't underestimate him. He was a policeman years ago in Taipei. He was working for the Wu-chai when he was a policeman. He's very clever, very determined."

Frank said, "How long has he been in Chicago?"

"Only five years. But he's making his mark."

Frank Chang sensed something. He said, "The Red Lantern Triad is in Chicago, aren't they?"

"They are," Chol Soo said.

But he did not elaborate. So . . . Frank thought, a city in the Midwest with two rival triads competing for something. Perhaps Chicago wasn't big enough for the both of them . . . well, it wasn't his place to know the why. He was just a Red Pole, after all.

Frank said, "What time is the flight?"

"Ten-thirty tonight."

"Okay," Frank said.

Fifteen minutes later he was on a train to Brooklyn. There would be time to visit his mistress before the plane left.

THREE

They started out the game with two tables, eight people at each one. The buy-in was five hundred dollars, so the total pot was eight thousand. They would divide it as they usually divided in Texas hold-'em, with sixty percent going to the winner, thirty percent to second place, and ten percent to third. The game didn't start right away . . . people drifting in the host's condo, chatting, checking in, and taking up the host's offer to get a beer out of the refrigerator. Most of the players were younger than Maitland, guys in their early to mid-thirties, though there was a fat guy with gray hair and a ponytail, more dirty than hippy, who said his name was Chet.

The fellow Maitland was with was a young lawyer named Jerry who liked to call people "dude" and "guy." Maitland had met him at a bar and bought him a beer and told him he was in Cleveland on business and had overheard the guy saying something about a card game. Maitland said he was dying of boredom, going to fucking meetings and seminars seven hours a day for almost a week now and he didn't know any chicks in Cleveland and, man, he needed something to *do.* Jerry said he could come along, but the buy-in was five hundred, and Maitland said that was cool with him.

It was a struggle at times. Maitland had turned forty a week earlier and he felt silly saying things like "cool" and "guy" and "babes," trying to sound young. But it was okay when he got there; he seemed normal and harmless enough to the others, looking white and middle class, and the host of the game told Maitland he was glad he had showed up as one of their usuals had bowed out this evening because his wife had told him he couldn't come. The host said, "You know how that is," and Maitland laughed with him, saying, yes, he did.

The games got underway, one game at each table.

He had been a good card player in his time. But his time was about eight years ago, back when he had been a patrolman with the Chicago PD. That had been before poker became a national craze. Also, when he had played, it had been seven-card stud more often than not and Texas hold-'em only occasionally. The winning hands were the same, but the betting strategy was different.

He played it conservatively for the first couple of hours, sipping water from a cup while the other guys drank and talked yuppie trash. There was a tall guy who looked like Ross from *Friends* who went on and on about an advertising account he was working on. Nobody really listened to him and he was the first to be chased out. Another guy fidgeted a great deal, taking off his sunglasses (though they were inside a condo at night) and putting them back on, doing the same with his ball cap, rattling his chips before folding, trying everybody's patience. He went out next after going all in on a pair of jacks against a king that came up in the flop, which inevitably paired up with someone else's king. Maitland's, fortunately. Then there were six and within a half-hour there were three, Maitland and a guy with a bright green shirt and a bright green tie and a skinny lady who kept barking out orders when she thought things were moving too slow, which was pretty much all the time. "Your action" and "come *on*," and so forth.

Maitland and these two joined the other table when it had dwindled down to four players. Their four and three from Maitland's table and now there were seven players left. Around one in the morning, it got down to four total and Maitland was still in it. Him, green shirt, the old hippy they called Chet, and a guy of about thirty who said his name was Bobby. The girl had been knocked out, her triple threes having lost to Maitland's trip sevens. She hung around anyway, still barking orders as if she were still in the game until the hippy turned on her and said, "Will you get the fuck out of here," and everyone laughed.

Around two A.M., green shirt got anxious and went all in on an unfilled flush and lost to the hippy. And then it was Maitland and, at worst, he'd go home with ten percent of the pot, eight hundred dollars. Three hundred profit when you subtract the five hundred, though there are better ways of passing five or six hours. The game settled into a different rhythm, perhaps more comfortable, perhaps just more fatigued. Cigarette smoke and beer had more or less permeated the condo now, but there were three guys and the girl still hanging around to see the outcome.

It was then that Maitland noticed the young guy called Bobby giving him a look. Trying to look for a tell and figure out if the new guy was bluffing. Maybe it was that.

During a shuffle, Bobby said to Maitland, "What'd you say your name was?"

"Evan," Maitland said.

"Where you from?"

"Chicago."

"What line are you in, Evan?"

"Financial planning. I work for American Express."

"In town for business?" Bobby said.

"Yeah."

Bobby was still looking at him. He said, "You look tired."

Maitland shrugged. "It is late."

"Don't worry," Bobby said. "You'll be out soon."

Maitland gave a small smile to the table, though he wouldn't make eye contact with the boy. He didn't merit that.

Hippie Chet was getting tired too. He went all in on an inside straight that never filled, his fatigue affecting his judgment. Then he was out and it was Maitland and Bobby. There were five guys standing around the table, the adrenaline of gambling and nicotine still with them. They wanted to see how it turned out, even the host, who had hoped to be in bed two hours ago.

Maitland said, "Can we take a break?"

Bobby said, "Yeah, that's fine. Five minutes." He was giving orders now. Maitland ignored him.

Maitland went to the bathroom and washed his face. Pushed his hands back into his blond hair, let the moisture stay there. He thought, three more hands. Three more and he would go all in. If he won, great. If not, that was fine too. Thirty percent would put twenty-four hundred in his pocket. It wouldn't be as much as forty-eight hundred, but he hadn't come here to win a game. He wanted to be back in Chicago by sunrise and it was looking like it would be more like lunchtime if he didn't get on with it.

It had left him sometime during the years. The competitive streak had been taken out of him, perhaps replaced by something else. Eight, nine years ago he would have wanted to beat this punk so badly it would have hurt. Second would have been better than third, but still a complete disappointment because Bobby drug dealer or some other punk would have been first and that would have been too much to bear. It happens to men who compete. When they're in it, when they're doing it and then, often suddenly, it's just gone. Age, indifference, fatigue . . . maybe just boredom. They don't want to play anymore. Mark Maguire doesn't want to hit any more home runs, Barry Sanders gets tired of running into the end zone, Zidane head-butts a mouthy Italian in the chest and walks off the field and into retirement.

As for Evan Maitland, the charm of sitting with young guys amidst smoke and chatter and the intoxicant of gambling was lost on him. He wanted to go home, take a shower, and get in bed.

Maitland opened the bathroom door and walked out. Bobby was waiting there. Maitland gave him a nod as he walked past and went into the bathroom.

Maitland waited.

Heard the flush of the toilet and then the taps come on as the guy washed his hands.

The door opened and Maitland was still in the hall waiting.

It was then that Bobby's expression changed. *Why was this guy still here?* Faggot or what? But, no, his spidey-sense was smarter than that. Drug dealers learn to become paranoid over time and often for good reason.

Maitland said, "You're name's not really Bobby, is it?"

A flicker in the man's eyes. Alarm.

"Sure it is," he said. "What's your fucking problem?"

Maitland took a folded piece of paper

from his jacket pocket. And the guy knew what it was even before Maitland unfolded it.

"Fuck," he said.

Maitland said, "Jeffrey Bauer. You skipped out on a bond."

"That's not me," Jeffrey said. For that was his real name.

"It is you. Jeff, your parents used their RV as collateral to get Mister Mead to put up your bond. You don't come back, Mead gets the RV. And he doesn't want an RV. He's already got one."

Jeffrey Bauer started to move past Maitland. Maitland shoved him back with one hand, knocking him against the bathroom door. Jeffrey stayed there, scared now. He wasn't a fighter and they both knew it.

Using cop's voice, Maitland said, "What do you think you're doing?" Often an authoritative voice and a small demonstration of violence were sufficient to gain control.

Jeffrey Bauer said, "Come on, man. I'm not a criminal. We got money on the table in there. It's my money. Okay, maybe it's your money too. You're not going to take me away now, are you?"

Maitland felt no sympathy for him. He was a punk and a coward and he felt no remorse that his parents were going to lose their RV because of him. Typical mid-level drug dealer.

Jeffrey said, "Come on, man. I was just selling pot, for Christ's sake. You want to put me in jail for that?"

"I don't care what you did, Jeffrey. But you made a promise to Charlie Mead that you would be present for trial and you didn't keep it. That's why I'm taking you back to Chicago."

Jeffrey straightened, but moved back a step. Getting ready to be brave. He said, "How about I tell those guys out there you're trying to kidnap me. You think they'll let you take me away?"

"I have no doubt they'll let me. You're not in a gangster's home, Jeffrey. It's a bunch of white guys playing cards. I'll flash my badge and my gun and they'll scatter." Maitland said, "You want to call me on *that,* go ahead."

And now Jeffrey Bauer's lower lip was trembling. He was beginning to cry.

And Maitland thought, oh, shit. For he'd seen it before. You catch them and they cry. They cry far more often than they fight. Particularly soft types like this one.

Maitland said, "Come on, don't do that. We'll get you back to Chicago and you'll see your lawyer and you'll get this whole thing straightened out."

"I don't want to go to jail. I can't go to jail." Sobbing now, he was broken and small.

"It'll work out," Maitland said, lying now to try to get past this moment. Maitland said, "Listen. We got a good game going in there. Let's go back and finish it. Maybe you'll win. Then we'll walk to my car and drive home. No one here will have to know."

Jeffrey Bauer sniffed twice, getting his composure back. Then he said, "Do you really have a gun?"

"Yeah," Maitland said, pulling his jacket back, exposing a .38 snubnose revolver. "It's right here."

"And you really won't tell those guys why you're here."

"You have my word."

"Okay," Jeffrey said.

They started to go back to the game. Then Jeffrey stopped.

"Hey," he said. "I've got an idea."

Maitland saw it coming. "Yeah?" he said, a smile on his face. Drug dealers were eternal squirrels.

"You let me go," Jeffrey said, "and I'll let you win the pot. I'll go all in on a shit hand and you win sixty percent of eight thousand dollars. It's more money than you'd get for bringing me in."

"Not quite," Maitland said. His fee was five grand on this one. "Besides, I'd be aiding and abetting a fugitive, and I don't do that sort of thing."

"Okay, then. I'll give you *all* of it."

"I don't think it's yours to give," Maitland said. "Listen, I've got a better idea. We go back and finish the game. Because you're in an emotional state, you're at a bit of a disadvantage. So if I win, we'll split it fifty-fifty. You win, you get the first place percentage."

Jeffrey Bauer said, "You'd do that?"

"Sure. But this is a good faith offer, Jeffrey. You get cute and try to run away from me, I'll shoot you in the back. Understand?"

Maitland was right. He did have an advantage over Jeffrey. It's difficult for a man to concentrate when he's facing jail and is conscious of a .38 snubnose revolver under the table. He tried though. Betting everything on what should have been a good hand: pair of kings in his hand and one up on the flop. No more kings coming up after that and Maitland hit a spade on the fourth card and made his flush.

Maitland kept his word though. They said their goodbyes and got out to the car — a 1975 Pontiac Catalina — and Maitland gave

Jeffrey enough money so that the split was even, $7,200 split two ways, hippy Chet having taken his ten percent. Maitland handcuffed Jeffrey's hands to the steering wheel and told him he could drive until they got to Indiana.

FOUR

It was almost noon before Maitland got back to his apartment. He lived on the north side, near Wrigley Field. His apartment was a modest two bedroom on a second-floor walk-up, but he had a two-car garage. He parked the Pontiac next to a silver 2001 BMW 740i Sport. A contrast between the two, the ugly Detroit workhorse next to the sleek autobahner. But he had lost two good cars doing bounty hunting work and he didn't want to lose any more.

Charlie Mead, the bondsman, had sold him the Pontiac for eight hundred bucks. The paint was faded and it needed a new set of rear coil springs and control arms, but the engine was good and the interior as well kept as widow's furniture. If the car got damaged by a cranked-out jumper, it would be no loss to Maitland. Besides, it was quick for a big car and the dual exhaust made a nice rumble.

Maitland locked the garage and walked up the fire escape steps to his apartment. Outside the back door, there was a charcoal cooker that was chained to the fire escape. It had not been used in three years. Julie's bicycle was chained nearby. She liked to ride along the lake on the weekends. She once asked Maitland if he'd like to buy one as well. He said he'd rather not.

Julie Ciskowski was a detective with the Chicago PD. They had met when she had been assigned to investigate a shooting wherein Maitland lost a lung. She later saved his life. She was a beautiful woman, petite and fair skinned, but a warrior underneath. She still had her own apartment, but most nights she spent at his place.

Maitland unlocked the back door, looking at her bike as he did so.

It's Saturday, he thought. Jesus, it's Saturday. He'd been in Cleveland for two days. Going on a tip and knowledge that the jumper couldn't resist a card game. But it'd taken him two days to track the guy down.

Julie should be off today. She wasn't here, and she wasn't riding her bicycle. Maybe she was at her own apartment. Maybe she was shopping. Maybe she was called in on a homicide. She was all right. She would call him if something was wrong.

Maitland took a shower. Dried off then got into a pair of undershorts and a T-shirt. He turned on the television in the living room and found a golf game. Johnny Miller commentary giving a nice lull to the summer afternoon. Half hour of that and Maitland went to his bed and lay down and put a pillow over his eyes. He was asleep in five minutes.

He awoke four hours later. Keys jingling in the back door. His eyes opening and closing as the bedroom ceiling came into view. A *thack* as the set of keys landed on the kitchen table.

Then Julie was standing in the bedroom door.

"Hey," Maitland said.

"Hey."

She was wearing jeans and a black T-shirt. No gun on her belt. Maitland supposed that was on the kitchen table as well.

She said, "When did you get back?"

"Around noon."

"You find him?"

"Yeah. He was playing cards."

"And it went okay?"

"Yeah. He didn't put up a struggle."

"Usually, they don't."

"Usually," Maitland said.

She remained in the doorway. She said, "Are you going back to sleep?"

"No, I don't think so. You want to come in here with me?"

Julie smiled. "Maybe. Will you take me out to dinner tonight?"

"Making conditions, are we?"

"Always. Besides, you made some money today."

Maitland said, "I'll take you anywhere you want."

"Okay," Julie said. She undid her belt and slid her pants down around her ankles. Then she stepped out of them. White panties contrasting with her black shirt as she walked over to the bed. She lifted the sheet and got underneath.

"My," she said. "You're a healthy devil, aren't you?"

Taking her in his arms, Maitland said, "I won thirty-six hundred dollars in a poker game." He had to tell somebody.

While Maitland and his girlfriend made love on the north side, a party was taking place on the south side of Lincoln Park. A Georgian-style mansion on a corner, about six blocks back from Lake Michigan. It was late afternoon and a light wind coming off the water made it ten degrees cooler than the western suburbs. A limousine parked out front that no one was going to move anytime soon. Valet parking for the other guests, their Mercedeses and Lexuses parked at a nearby lot. Inside, Chicago's beautiful people.

Bianca Garibaldi did not consider herself a part of Chicago society. She was comfortably well off, but not of extreme wealth. This was not a concern to her. She came to these things when she was invited for a couple of reasons. First, because her husband Max enjoyed them and, second, because it helped her get business. Her Italian accent and her elegant good looks were an asset in that regard, and that was okay with her. She was co-owner of Colette's Antiques, specializing in 17th- and 18th-century French and Italian furnishings. So the sign said at her boutique in Evanston. Her partner was a former policeman named Evan Maitland.

Maitland had a good eye for the merchandise and it gave him no shame to tell people he sold furniture for a living. Bianca did not like it when he would take time off to chase a criminal who had jumped bail. She thought Evan had some issues and maybe some growing up to do and, like too many American men, was somehow attracted to

38

violence. He had told her, more than once, that she was wrong about this as she was often wrong about him. He told her he hated violence, but he loved to hunt and there was a difference. Bianca didn't see it.

Bianca Garibaldi came from Milano to Chicago a little over twenty years ago to attend Northwestern University. She studied art and upon graduating took a job as a buyer for an upscale department store. Got bored with the travel after a few years and moved back to Italy for approximately eight months. She was glad to be back . . . at first, but then soon came to realize that being an independent, ambitious Italian woman wasn't as easy as it seemed. At least not in Italy. Age and sex discrimination were routine practices there, barely hidden, and the government was corrupt and, with its despicable kowtowing to the Cosa Nostra thugs, seemed determined to ruin what had once been a great nation and a great culture. To her surprise, she felt out of place. So she returned to Chicago and got into the antique business. In time, she accepted her role as a European woman residing in America.

Now, she and Max were engaged in a conversation with a real estate developer and his wife. It had been going on only a few minutes, but the wife was wearing Bianca out. Talking about how the Episcopalian church began, getting a lot of it wrong, but Bianca wouldn't bother to correct her. There would be no point in that. The woman was giving all her eye contact to Max as she prattled on. Another overly competitive American woman, pushing up her enormous, implanted air tits. It wouldn't be so bothersome if the woman had some sexual interest in Max, but it was about attention, not sex.

Meanwhile, the husband was staring at Bianca as if she were something he had just bought off a porn rack. Like she had no eyes of her own and wouldn't notice his leers. Bianca thought he was gross, perhaps even unbalanced. She reminded herself that she shouldn't be surprised. You come to these things thinking you'll see Dick Powell and Myrna Loy bon vivance, but it never quite turns out that way.

Still, it was a big deal. The Mayor was here, working the crowd by letting it drift to him. He was gracious and never complained when someone asked if he wouldn't mind being photographed with them. Congressman Tasset was here too with his platinum-blonde wife. The former Miss Illinois, now co-hosting *Good Morning Chicago.* The buzz of wealth and power and access.

A couple of days earlier, Bianca had told Maitland that he should come too and to bring Julie with him. Messing with him a bit when she said it, Maitland responding, "Those things bore me to tears."

"But you're a salesman," she said. "Those people are our best clients, whether you like them or not."

And Maitland said, "What was it Mac Davis said in *North Dallas Forty*? 'We're all whores anyway.'"

Bianca said, "I never saw that."

"One of the best movies ever made."

"About football?"

"About life."

"So going to this party would make you a whore?"

"Yes."

"You're full of shit. You just don't want to go."

"You're right about that."

"And for the worst reason, too."

"What's that?"

"You're a snob."

"Am I?"

"The worst sort. A middle-class snob. You look down on almost everyone. You still think of criminals as 'turds.' You think of the rich as bores. Which select few of us get

41

to pass your test?"

"You, for a start."

"Right. Go to Cleveland and shoot some people."

Now the big-chested woman was asking her something.

Bianca said, "Pardon?"

"Have you met him?"

"Met who?"

"Preston Wong. The man who owns this place."

"Yes," Bianca said. "We met him when we got here."

"You know," the woman said, "he doesn't have an accent or anything. I mean, he talks like us."

Max said, "Well, he's not from China."

The woman did not lower her voice. "I *know* that," she said, irritated now. Bianca wondered how many glasses of wine the woman had had.

Her husband said, "He's from San Francisco. He moved to Chicago about five years ago. Very smart, very smart." Nodding his head when he said it.

Bianca thought "very smart" was code for "very rich and very Oriental." Yellow skin, but *gud-damn* he's got some money. She remembered a black friend of hers once telling her that if you were black, you would be presumed stupid until you proved you were smart, but if you were Asian, it was the other way around.

The real estate developer's wife said, "His wife is beautiful. She's wearing that kimono."

And Max waited a moment before saying, "I don't think it's actually a kimono."

It was then that Bianca saw Alexis Sutherland motioning to her.

"Excuse me," Bianca said.

Alexis Sutherland was a woman of about fifty. She co-owned a real estate business with her husband, the two of them working as a sort of tag team and making tremendous profits. She was good natured as well as smart and she had been a regular client of Bianca's for years. She was standing with an Asian man as Bianca walked up.

She said, "Bianca, this is the man I was telling you about."

He was a Chinese-American of about forty-five. Handsome and well-groomed. He extended a hand and said, "Raymond Liu."

"Hi. Bianca Garibaldi."

He said, "Alexis said you wanted to discuss some Chinese objects."

"Yes. If you don't mind."

"Not at all. Would you like to sit down?"

"Yes. Thank you."

They took a seat on a divan and Alexis said she'd leave them alone. Bianca heard her bark out a laugh to someone else. She smiled to herself.

Liu said, "Have you known Alexis long?"

"For almost ten years," Bianca said. "She is one of my best clients."

"I've been in the antique business for about that long. It's funny we've not met before."

"Well," Bianca said, "we're selling different things. Generally, we stay with French and Italian antiques. But my partner — do you know Evan?"

"Who?"

"Evan Maitland. He's my partner."

"Your husband?"

"No. My business partner."

"Ah. No, I don't know him."

"Well, he was in Los Angeles a couple of weeks ago on a buying trip and he didn't turn up anything that we normally sell. So he had some time to kill and he went to an estate sale from this woman who had died. I don't remember her name. But she was Chinese or Korean. She had an American last name, though. The estate was in Pasadena at an upscale home, so he took a chance. Anyway, he saw a display cabinet there that he picked up for . . . not much money. We had it authenticated there. It's from the Ming dynasty."

"A display cabinet?"

"Yes."

"With the *Huali* wood?"

"Yes."

"Ah. That's quite a find. From the seventeenth century. I wouldn't mind having that in my inventory."

Bianca smiled. "Sorry, we've already found a buyer."

"So I thought."

"You're familiar with the piece, though?"

"Yes. I believe it has four gold hinges and a clasp in the middle, a little sword through the hole?"

"Yes. Yes, that's right." She was impressed now, feeling better that she'd gotten in touch with this man. She said, "And there's an upper section above that. Above the doors. It's open."

"The display space."

"Yes."

"I see. And has your buyer items to place there?"

"No."

Raymond Liu said, "We can make an appointment."

"That would be fine," Bianca said. "But my client has an idea of what she wants already."

"She does?" Liu said.

"Yes," Bianca said. She knew it was uncommon for a client to have specific knowledge of foreign antiques. She said, "Are you familiar with something called the Chenghua chicken cups?"

"The chicken cups," Liu said. "Oh, yes. I know them very well."

"Also from the Ming dynasty?"

"Yes. They're painted in the technique known as the 'dovetailing colors.' I won't ask you to reveal your client's identity, but if she knows of this, I am most impressed. Tell me, has she inquired about a wooden stand?"

"Yes, as a matter of fact."

"Then she must know it."

"She wants both a cup and an original wooden stand. And she's willing to pay for it. Presuming they're authentic."

"Of course."

Bianca said, "Can you help me?"

Liu said, "I can. But I'll tell you that I don't have one now. I know where I can get one. And we can have an independent expert authenticate that it's from the Ming period and that it's Chenghua. She would have to pay for that, of course."

"I understand."

"I have contacts all over China. And I think that within a couple of days, I would at least have some photographs that we can examine. Would that be acceptable to you?"

"Yes." Bianca pulled a card out of her purse and handed it to him.

Raymond Liu smiled when he took it. He said, "I must warn you, the wooden stand may be more difficult. Many of the originals were discarded, the first owners not having realized their worth. But . . . that's a common problem in the antique business, isn't it?"

"Yes," Bianca said. "Do you think you'll know something by Monday afternoon?"

"I believe so."

They stood and Liu gave her a slight bow, but took her hand as well, mixing east and west. "Until then, Ms. Garibaldi."

Raymond Liu watched the woman walk back to her husband. Hmmm. She had a nice backside. He was not normally a pursuer of women, but there was something exotic about Bianca Garibaldi. She was not Chinese and she was not American. Liu had reached an age where he had become bored with Chinese wives and with Chinese prostitutes. It had not always been this way with him. He had left Hong Kong when he was still a teenager and relocated to the south side of Chicago. Lonely, awful times. His father working for coolie wages, his mother scrubbing floors for even less. He thought his own fate was worse. School with blacks and whites and not a Chinese in sight. The girls scorned him, the blacks and whites came together in a show of racial unity to loathe him. *Chink, yellow-dog, gook, viet cong.* Kids saying he was like that gook in the Robert De Niro movie that made the American soldiers play Russian Roulette. Liu told them that was Vietnam, not China. It made no difference. They were intent on bullying him.

Eventually he drifted into a gang. The Wolf Boys. They taught him martial arts and gave him a sense of belonging. Chinese youths who looked like him, talked like him, felt like him. They were homesick like him. And not just for China, but for Chinese girls.

But the boy becomes a man and his tastes change. Raymond Liu did not remain with the Wolf Boys much beyond the age of twenty. It was around that time that he was approached by the Red Lantern Triad. Their recruiter told him he was too smart to be doing home invasions and holding up liquor stores and getting in stupid turf fights with black gangsters. Did he want to remain a *li-*

ang jie, a punk? The recruiter, whose name had been Ho, eventually steered Liu away from the Wolf Boys and into university and before Liu had completed his first year, he had already sworn the 36 Oaths of the Red Lantern. An exchange that he had never regretted.

By the age of twenty-five, the transformation was complete. No more jean jackets or headbands or conspicuous tattoos. Instead, it was tailored suits, Swiss watches, a Mercedes. They set him up with a store. Chinese antiques and objects. He would sell these goods to the public. He would mingle and become accepted in white American society. He would run an operation that laundered drug profits for the Red Lantern Triad. This task was both acceptable and desirable to Raymond Liu.

Now he had a Chinese wife, one they had more or less given him. Delivered from Hong Kong. The Red Lantern was skeptical of American-born Chinese women. *Tow Gee,* they called them. Liu's wife's name was Fei Xe. Liu had three children with her.

Raymond Liu could not refuse such a gift from the Red Lantern. But his was not a monogamous nature. He had had two mistresses over the years. Chinese women, one a *Tow Gee,* the other from Shanghai. And

49

there had been a few prostitutes as well. More white American women than Chinese as the years passed.

He had noticed Bianca Garibaldi even before he was introduced to her. And when he was up close, her perfume and her voice as well as her look had captivated him.

But she's no fool, he thought. He would have to proceed cautiously. Carefully. The first thing would be to get her alone. Invite her to the apartment that he kept in the city, apart from his house in Oak Park. As the Chinese said, the clever hare always keeps more than one nest.

FIVE

Oliver Nagel did not mind being called a mercenary. He would do his best for whatever candidate retained him. But he was loyal to his party and loyal to the end to those he worked for. Even after the campaign was finished and years in the past, he would never be openly critical of the candidate he had hustled for. This code he maintained even when a cowardly politician blamed everyone but himself for his loss. *I should have kept closer to my own personal vision, instead of listening to my advisors.* That sort of cheap shit.

He had been hired by Tasset six months earlier. Congressman Joe Tassett had held the ninth congressional seat for the last three terms, but he had drawn a savvy opponent this election and he didn't want to take any chances. Nagel himself was concerned by the challenger. An impassioned young African American lawyer who spoke and presented well and didn't have any skeletons they could find. Joe, who should've known better, said that maybe the guy wasn't much of a threat because he didn't seem to have much money.

Nagel said, "If there's one thing I've learned in this business, it's this: a candidate with a lot of money, but no coherent message or grassroots campaign will lose to a candidate with a great message and a great grassroots campaign. Because the candidate with the great message and the great organization will eventually *raise* the money. Buying a congressional seat ain't as easy as it seems."

But Joe Tasset was an incumbent. And though that was a distinct advantage, it was no guarantee of victory. They still needed support. And they still needed money. Advertising, polling, opposition research, campaign staff, and legal fees. Oliver Nagel's retainer was $15,000 a month alone. It added up, and quick.

Now Nagel said, "You've been generous to us in the past. We haven't forgotten that."

Preston Wong considered this and made a gesture. Then he said, "I support the policies of the Congressman. And his party. I don't think of that as generosity. I consider that good citizenship."

"Of course," Nagel said.

"I do too," Congressman Tasset said. "But I look upon it as friendship as well."

Preston Wong nodded.

Nagel said, "But as you know, this is a continuing process. Avery Wyatt is a formidable opponent."

Wong said, "You are concerned, then?"

"I wouldn't say concerned," Nagel said. "But in my business, we say that it's best to run scared."

They had left the party to discuss politics in Preston Wong's office in his home. The Congressman, his chief political operative, and Preston Wong, owner of the Oriental Bank of Chicago and president of the Pacific Commodities Group. Three men of power, though each of them from different backgrounds and contrasting appearances.

Joe Tasset had been a football coach before going into politics. He was a man of bulk and his suits never seemed to drape the right way. Inoffensive, unimaginative, affable, and comfortably good looking. Bankable personality traits in a politician.

Oliver Nagel was originally from Brooklyn, went to law school at NYU, practiced law for four months, and quit before he went crazy from boredom. He had been working in campaigns ever since.

Preston Wong had come from San Francisco a few years earlier. A man of wealth and taste. Of almost slight build, he favored Italian suits, but avoided the high-dollar watches. He had been taught from a young age that ostentation was unbecoming. Enough, but not too much. That was the key.

Preston Wong said, "Of course you have my support. My continued support."

"We know that," Nagel said.

"But perhaps it is not enough." Wong did not make it a question.

There was a silence among them for a moment. Then Nagel said, "Well . . ."

Wong raised a hand, signaling that he had meant no offense. He said, "These are important issues. Important to Chicago and our state. But I think we're sometimes shortsighted."

Congressman Tasset said, "What do you mean?"

"Do you want to remain a Congressman?"

Tasset said, "For now, yes. I've thought about Senate, if the seat becomes available. Maybe governor."

"Or ambassador," Wong said. "Perhaps to China." He was smiling now.

"Yeah, maybe," Tasset said, forcing a laugh into it. He was hiding his discomfort.

"Well," Wong said, "all things in time." He turned to Nagel. "I think we should have a fundraiser. Conservatively, we should be able to raise three million."

Nagel had been hoping for two, at best. He said, "Three million? You could do that?"

"Without question. It's a fair goal, isn't it?"

"Yes," Tasset said. He was barely able to suppress his joy.

"The Hyatt Regency," Wong said. "I think that would be the best place. We'll work out the details later." Wong stood, signaling that their meeting was over. "Gentlemen, please feel welcome in my home anytime."

The guests were gone and Wong telephoned Hsu-shen.

In Cantonese, Wong said, "Are they assembled?"

"Yes. All here."

"Okay," Wong said and hung up the phone.

He had his assistant bring the car around to the front of the house, a black Jaguar XJ8. Wong got behind the wheel and drove down Lake Shore Drive. The sun was setting now, coming off the lake and giving the skyscapers on the shore their golden hue.

He passed Oak Street Beach and the Drake Hotel, made the arc out past the John Hancock building, and continued south. Fifteen minutes later, he was on Tan Court Road, coming into Chinatown.

He pulled the Jaguar up to the door of a warehouse and honked the horn three times. He looked up through the windshield at a closed-circuit camera, an eye looking back and the door opened.

He parked the car and walked toward Hsu-shen.

Hsu-shen was about thirty, fifteen or so years younger than Wong. Wong had recruited him to the Wu-Chai when Hsu-shen was still a teenager. He had been discovered at a local martial arts club. Their champion even at that age. Hsu-shen was loyal, compact, and deadly. Wong had once seen a big redneck poke Hsu-shen in the chest. Then Hsu-shen's hand and arm were a blur, a bolt of lightning shooting out to the redneck's temple, back at Hsu-shen's side before the redneck had even hit the ground. The strike had killed him. When Wong had left San Francisco for Chicago, he had brought Hsu-shen with him.

Hsu-shen wore jeans and a sportcoat. Beneath his shirt, his back was covered with the tattoo of a dragon. His hair was pulled back in a ponytail.

Wong said, "They're all here?"

"Yes. Sik-ho got here last. His flight was delayed."

"Okay," Wong said. "He's one of the 49s."

"Yes."

"And the Red Pole?"

"He's here. Got here late last night."

"Good."

Wong was pleased. Two 49s, ordinary members, and a Red Pole. He had not wanted three men of the same rank. It could lead to trouble if there was no leadership. It had been a problem when he was a policeman as well as with the Wu-Chai Triad. The Red Pole from New York, the 49s from Hong Kong and Vancouver, respectively. If it went well, they would all be out of Chicago in forty-eight hours and back in their own cities. He did not want his own men directly involved.

They were waiting for them in a bare storage room. Two of them sitting in the folding metal chairs, the third leaning against the wall with a cigarette in his mouth. Upon Wong and Hsu-shen's entry, the two got out of their chairs. A moment passed before the third detached himself from the wall, a look passing between him and Hsu-shen.

Wong said, "Sit down."

The three men took seats. Wong remained standing, comfortable with his place and position. He said, "You may know each other already." He pointed with his chin, as the Chinese do, each of them in turn.

"Chang, Yu-shi, and Sik-ho." New York, Hong Kong, Vancouver.

Wong said, "You are here to assassinate two men of the Red Lantern Triad. You have been selected, in part, because you are not tied to or loyal to the Red Lantern. If any of you feels this job will violate your respective oaths, you may leave now. If not, we will continue."

Sik-ho looked at the other two men, a slight smile on his face. Nobody said anything.

"Good," Wong said. "The two men are not high officers of the Red Lantern. We are not starting a war with them. We are simply sending them a message. I do not want either of these targets mutilated or tortured. That is not allowed. You will simply dispose of them. You will report to Hsu-shen when it is done. He will not accompany you. When these jobs are finished, you will each be paid $50,000. And you will each leave town. You will not stay in Chicago afterward to gamble or to have a woman. You will leave town when the job is done. Chang will be your leader, as he is of higher rank in his society than you are in yours. This is my decision, not his."

Wong signaled to Hsu-shen. Hsu-shen brought him a manila envelope. Wong removed from the envelope two photographs. He said, "These are the targets. The first is Robert Wo. He is the Red Lantern's chemist. He is your first priority."

Wong replaced this photo with another.

He said, "The second target is this man. His name is Raymond Liu."

Six

They ate dinner at the Berghoff, sitting at a table near the sign that said, "Vote for Pete Bartzen Vote — Twice." Remnant of Chicago in the Twenties.

Maitland said, "Do you know that that guy had Marshal Field's surrounded by police with machine guns? They wouldn't let anybody out until Field started building a fire escape."

"Compassionate conservatism," Julie said.

"Depends on how you look at it. That was back when the Democratic Machine ruled this city."

"Don't they still?"

Maitland said, "You're a cynic."

"Maybe," Julie said. "I don't know."

"Is something wrong?"

She hesitated a moment. Then said, "Oh, I don't know. Work . . . you know."

"What?"

"The sergeant's promotion is coming up."

"Are you on the list?"

"Yeah. There's three other women and about a dozen men. They'll give one of the slots to a woman. You know how it works."

"You do well on the exam?"

"Yes. But that's only part of it. There's the interview too."

"Done that yet?"

"No."

"Who's on the panel?"

"Tom Phillips, Deke Holt, and some guy from the insurance fraud unit . . . Lanier."

"I remember Phillips, vaguely."

"He's okay, but Holt's pretty tight with Ben Cason."

There was a silence, Julie looking not at him, but across the dining room.

"Oh," Maitland said.

The mood changed then. And he felt it from her. Not anger or resentment, but an answer to his question. He had asked her what was bothering her and she had told him.

When they had met, she was a detective working under the supervision of Captain Ben Cason. A police officer who was not necessarily corrupt or mean, but a little on the weak side and indecisive. An old school boy who liked his wife and liked his daughters, but unconsciously thought of women

61

cops as either little girls to be protected or ball-busting bitches. He had Julie Ciskowski figured as the cute daughter type, the sort he could take under his wing and help out here and there with his fatherly wisdom. When she didn't sustain that illusion, he felt what he would have called disappointment. Julie, understandably, saw it different.

Over a year ago, she was assigned to investigate a shooting that had taken place in Oklahoma City, but whose participants came from and resided in Chicago. The chief surviving victim of the shooting was Evan Maitland, having lost a lung in the gunfight. She had been told at the outset that he used to be a Chicago cop who had worked undercover in narcotics and that he left under a cloud. She was told that he had taken money from a drug dealer and then killed him when the guy threatened to expose him. She had been told that Maitland was a dirty cop who got lucky and didn't get popped, but now there was a chance to get him after all. She had been told this not by Ben Cason, but by Terry Specht, an internal affairs investigator.

Julie did her work, interviewed Maitland, chased down leads. His story about the Oklahoma City shooting checked out and his story about the past checked out too. It had been a clean shoot and he had been cleared by a neutral arbitrator. In other words, he had not been terminated from the Chicago PD. Rather, he had resigned after being cleared, having determined that his enemies would ensure that he would receive no more promotions or decent assignments.

When she made her report to Cason, Terry Specht was in Cason's office. To Julie, this itself was a small betrayal. She reported to Cason, not Specht. She told them that Maitland was clean and that she didn't think Specht had the objectivity to be involved in this investigation. Or to interfere with it.

Cason sided with Specht, indeed scolded her for showing Specht disrespect. He did not change his position even when Specht implied that Julie had slept with Maitland. (She hadn't at that time.) Julie didn't back down. She did not amend her report. And when it was over, she told Cason she would not file a complaint against him or Specht if he granted her request for a transfer to work under another supervisor.

Cason, who still didn't get it, said, "Complaint? What for?"

"For implying that I was screwing a material witness, to begin with."

Cason granted her request, all the while shaking his head and saying he regretted it had come to this. Like it was her fault.

Julie would later tell Maitland, "I hope you understand I didn't do that for you. It wasn't about you."

It was about her. Terry Specht had tried his damnedest to get Maitland fired years earlier. It didn't work and he wanted Julie to help him retaliate. Specht was a stupid, petty, mean-spirited bully wanting to exact vengeance. Such men were not uncommon in police departments, but Julie had never gotten over the fact that Cason had sided with him instead of her.

Was it because she was a woman? Did they laugh to each other after she walked out of Cason's office, one of them telling the other, "Must be that time of the month." Heh-heh. Was it because she hadn't played the part of the clueless little girl in need of paternal guidance? Wouldn't say things like, "Well, what do you guys think?"

Maitland had said it had probably started before she had investigated him. Before that, she had killed a man armed with a machine gun on a train platform. A man who had killed two people and wounded a third before the first set of patrol officers showed

64

up. The tact team was on its way, but the maniac was still armed and holding innocent commuters at bay. Julie Ciskowski, at five foot five, borrowed another woman's coat and frumpy hat, went up the stairs, and merged herself into the crowd. Moved to the front of it and shot the man three times and killed him.

Heroic conduct for which she received an award. But not terribly helpful to a policewoman's career in the long term. Departmental murmurs, most of them male, that she should have waited for backup, that she got lucky, that she was a showboat, etc. It led to problems in her marriage too. Or revealed them.

Now Maitland said, "Well, maybe it won't make a difference."

Julie said, "You believe that?" Her voice a little sharp then. She could be very blunt at times.

Maitland shrugged.

"That's what I thought," she said.

"Sorry."

Julie sighed. "What are you sorry for?"

"I don't know."

"My relationship with you is not going to cost me the promotion."

"You sure?"

"Evan, it's not as if you're a criminal. You

have a handful of enemies in the department. No more than the average."

"You get asked about it?"

"Not so much. There's always someone making a pass, most of them married. Since my divorce and my taking up with you, it's like they think I'm open for business." She smiled. "Apparently if I'd sleep with you, I'd sleep with anybody." She said, "Listen."

"Yeah?"

"I'm not asking you to declare anything, okay? But I'd like to know . . . something."

"What do you mean?"

"I mean, where this is going."

"Oh, well —"

"You don't have to give me specifics, Evan. The divorce decree wasn't that long ago. And I'm in no hurry to rush into something else. It's just that . . ."

"Are you wanting to get married again?"

"No. Jesus. No. Listen, I don't even know if I want to ever be married again, at all. I may not be cut out for it."

"Then . . . what?"

"Forget it. I don't think it's a good idea to define the relationship."

"But you just said —"

"Forget what I said. I'm sorry I went on like this. I must be tired." She said, "Are you? From your trip, I mean?"

"Yeah, sort of."
"Let's go home then."

SEVEN

He was not surprised the next morning when she was dressed and out of bed before he awoke. Hearing footsteps hard on the wood floor when he opened his eyes. At least she wasn't tiptoeing around. Going back and forth from the kitchen to the bathroom, water running then not running, cabinets opening and closing. She came back in the bedroom, fully clothed.

"Hey," she said.

"Hey."

"I put some coffee on. I have to get going."

Maitland didn't ask where to. He was not the sort to keep tabs. He said, "Okay," his voice accepting.

"I'll call you later," Julie said.

"Sure. Have a good day."

"I will," she said. She walked over and kissed him quickly and then walked out.

He waited to hear the back door close

before he got out of bed.

He had been married once himself and he had at least learned that there was no understanding women. Define the relationship if you're of a mind, but don't ask too many questions at the wrong time because it'll usually get you nowhere. He'd read once that the key to a successful marriage was a mutual misunderstanding. Though it was a gay guy who'd said it.

Maitland put his bathrobe on and walked to the kitchen. The small coffeepot was about three quarters full. Maitland switched it off. A great lady, but she made awful coffee. Put in too many scoops and usually of the wrong stuff too. For her, there was no difference between generic brands and the high quality. For him, there was. Still, if she were here, he would have drunk it. Well . . . sipped half a cup before she left the room so he could pour it down the sink.

He put two slices of bread in the toaster and walked over to the window overlooking the courtyard. The trees and shrubs were green. It was supposed to get up to ninety degrees today, warm for a Chicago summer. Warm, but not hot. One of the good things about this city. He had lived here all his life and he was used to the long, cold winters and the short, pleasant summers.

Had visited Florida once and could not comprehend why anyone would ever want to retire there. Maybe thirty or so years from now he would join the ranks of the old men who died of heart attacks shoveling the first heavy snow off their walk. There could be worse fates than that.

He looked at the kitchen table. The *Sun-Times* was there. Julie had already brought it in from the back step. Nice of her. She was a nice, good lady. He felt guilty for being relieved that she had left.

Define the relationship. Christ, what does that mean? When he had been a policeman for a couple of years, he had thought he had learned that criminals never tell the truth. But as he got older, he started to wonder if anyone ever really told the truth. Not that they lied directly, but ever told the truth. Even knew the truth. How do you define a relationship? Tell her you love her and that you like being with her and like making love to her? What difference would it make?

He remembered his ex-wife renting a movie once that he didn't like very much. An American woman goes to Spain to research the *machismo* mystique. A fairly predictable woman's fantasy that ended with her getting the lay of her life. But there was one scene that Maitland liked. It was where the Spanish interpreter kept lying to her about the interviewee's responses to her questions. She catches him at it and the interviewer says, "What difference does it make? They're not giving you truthful answers anyway."

Because she was asking "relationship" questions. Sex, love, matters of the heart. Who can answer honestly about such things? The body can be honest about such matters, but words are another matter. The man makes a move and the woman responds with a passionate kiss and they go from there. That was about as honest a dialogue as you were ever going to get.

Maybe he was costing Julie a promotion to sergeant. Maybe that was what was bothering her. But he suspected that wasn't really the issue. Her problems were with him. She had been talking around it last night. Perhaps because she wanted to avoid conflict. More likely because she was a nice person who didn't want to upset him. He could push it forward, say to her, "If you want to end it, that's okay." But that might blow up in his face, her saying, "End it? That's not what I meant at all. Is that what you want? Is it?" And then they'd both be in that mess.

Ah, well, he was a coward then. Avoiding

"meaningful" dialogue same as her. Sometimes it was best to keep your mouth shut.

The telephone rang.

Maybe it was her. Calling him to say it
was over and could he be out of the apartment the next day while she came to get
her things? Sure, he could do that if she
wanted to . . . Christ, pick up the phone,
you pussy.

"Hello."

"Evan, it's Mead. You get the guy?"

"I got him. You got my money?"

Charlie Mead had the table manners of a
billy goat and Maitland was generally
reluctant to meet him for lunch. Mead was
a big man, a guy who had been a competitive athlete in high school and had let
himself go thereafter. But mentally he was
on top of things. He was the owner and
manager of Mead's Bail Bonds.

A few weeks ago, Jeffrey Bauer had sold
crystal methamphetamine to a police informant with a tape recording device in his
cell phone. The police swarmed Jeffrey as
he approached his car, guns drawn, young
cops saying *freeze, motherfucker,* yelling the
way cops yell, and they hustled him off to
jail. Jeffrey Bauer had been caught before.
He was a small-time dealer, not connected

to any sort of cartel or bigger outfit. A small fish in the neverending war on drugs. The judge set his bail at fifty thousand. Jeffrey's parents came to Charlie Mead. Mead told him he operated on good faith and collateral, which meant collateral, now. So the Bauers put up their recreational vehicle and Charlie dropped the keys and the title in his desk drawer. Jeffrey Bauer was, of course, aware of what his parents had done for him, but didn't give it much thought when he jumped bail and ran to Cleveland. Mead called the Bauers and told them he'd have to keep their RV, but that he'd rather not. He said for a fee of five thousand dollars, he could retain a bounty hunter who could probably track Jeffrey down and bring him back. The Bauers said if you think it's worth it and Mead said he thought it was.

Mead was waiting for Maitland at the parking lot of a Catholic church in the western part of the city. His wife was sitting in the passenger seat of a Buick station wagon and his three kids were running around the grass nearby, Mead leaning against the car smoking a cigar. Cars were leaving the parking lot after the ten o'clock mass.

Maitland parked his silver BMW and walked over.

Mead said, "Go to church this morning, Evan?"

Maitland shook his head. "My alarm clock's busted." He peered through the driver's side window at Mead's wife. "Hi, Estelle."

"Hi, Evan. You doing okay?"

"Better than I was yesterday."

Charlie Mead said, "We'll just be a second, okay?"

Estelle Mead said, "Don't take too long." She returned her attention to the church's weekly bulletin.

They walked a respectful distance away from the car and Mead handed him the cashier's check for five thousand dollars.

Mead said, "His parents wanted to know if you hurt him."

"Why would I do that?"

"I know you wouldn't," Mead said. "But his parents never met you. They hear 'bounty hunter' and they think you're some guy with tattoos and a bandanna."

"Ah, such prejudice," Maitland said. Some of the bounty hunters *did* have tattoos and bandannas. Some of them looked like off-duty mailmen. Most of them were just blokes though, who wanted to avoid violence as much as the next man. Maitland knew one, Emmit Stans, who was as tattooed as Jesse James, had a handlebar mustache, and at six-six towered over most men. His size was an advantage to be sure, as most jumpers would submit just at the sight of him. But he was a gentle person who didn't even like people to use foul language around him. When he caught a jumper who broke down crying in despair, it was not unusual for Emmit to take him by the hands and say a prayer with him to calm him down. Laugh if you like, but it worked more often than not.

For his part, Evan Maitland was an average-looking man who tended to resemble the role people saw him in. When he was selling antiques, he dressed that part and it became him. When he adopted a certain tone of voice and gave people like Jeffrey Bauer a firm shove, he became, to the other, a bounty hunter.

Mead wanted to know about Jeffrey Bauer, find out how Maitland tracked him down, and if there was any drama to it. Maitland told him about the card game. Mead shrugged, not that impressed or interested. Charlie Mead had never really been into cards or gambling. He had said "flop?" early in the story, not knowing what it meant, and Maitland realized he should have dropped it then.

75

Mead said, "I'm going to tell you about this thing, because I'm going to tell you. I mean, there's a lot of money in it. But I don't think you should get involved."

Maitland said, "What is it?"

"Do you know of a guy named Ricky Cannavaro?"

"Uh, is he part of Zanatelli's outfit?"

"Yeah, he's tied to it. He got popped on a drug thing and they set bail at three hundred thousand. They put up bond and he left town. He might be in New York. Or around Lake Tahoe. It'd be thirty thousand dollars if you brought him back."

"And you're giving me right of first refusal?"

"Yeah. And my advice is, refuse."

"Yeah, well, I appreciate that. But with or without your advice, I'd refuse. You know my rule."

"Yeah, I know it. I just wanted to tell you, that's all. Cannavero wants to stay gone, he can stay gone."

"What'd he put up as collateral?"

"His house. His wife's called three times now, yelling at me like it's my fault. But she probably knew better than anybody he was going to bolt. Or disappear."

"If she didn't, she should have," Maitland said.

Maitland's rule was that if it involved the mob, he was out. Cannavero was one of John Zanatelli's people and Zanatelli was old-school Cosa Nostra. He was in prison now, but he could still have people killed. For all he knew, Cannavero was dead already, buried in the Wisconsin woods. The American Mafia was a fading thing anyway, thriving more on HBO than in reality, but there were still remnants and Maitland had found it was best to let others poke that hornet's nest.

Now that he had turned down the job, Mead seemed in better spirits.

Maitland said, "What do you think will happen to Bauer?"

"You getting soft, Evan?"

"Well, he cried on me. And I've always kind of wanted a son."

Mead laughed. "Heaven help us, Father Flanagan; there *is* such a thing as a bad boy. Well, he'll probably get a two-year rec. If he's smart, he'll take it, 'cause they've got him cold. State prison, so he'd probably get out in eight or nine months. Then you can buy him a coke and take him to a ball game."

"Maybe it'll straighten him out," Maitland said.

"I doubt it," Mead said. "So I guess you'll

just stick with the furniture, huh?"

"For the time being," Maitland said. "But call me in a month or so. I might get restless again."

EIGHT

Robert Wo had learned his craft from Lee Man-kwan, the premier heroin chemist of Shanghai. The Red Lantern had sent him there fifteen years ago for that express purpose. When the old man died, Wo felt it was permissible to improve upon what had up till then been considered perfection. It was not. For there is no perfection and never was. What there was was stretching the limits to attain the highest purity. In his time, Lee Man-kwan had no equal. With proper backing from the most powerful triad in mainland China, he had produced No. 4 heroin of 92% purity. But that was in the eighties. And after the master died, Robert Wo used what he had learned from Lee and went on his own to make it better. By the mid-nineties, he had succeeded. Wo's heroin No. 4 was of 94% purity, arguably the best in the country.

Accordingly, he was important to the Red

Lantern. With him at all times were two bodyguards. This he had in spite of holding no official title in the Red Lantern. Robert Wo was not a Red Pole or even a 49. He was not a soldier in their army. He was a master chemist, as important to the livelihood of the Red Lantern as the German rocket scientists had once been to NASA.

Robert Wo did not gamble or drink. He had no wife and, indeed, had rarely ever expressed interest in any woman. At fifty-eight years of age, he was something of a secular monk. He liked Chinese art and he liked the symphony. He did not think in terms of right or wrong or the destruction of heroin addiction. He enjoyed living comfortably and he enjoyed the respect and the position that his talent had brought him.

Frank Chang had learned all these things about Wo before he set out to kill him.

It was about eight o'clock in the evening when the North Line of the Metra Union Pacific pulled to a stop at the west gate of the Ravinia Festival. It was about twenty miles north of downtown Chicago. Light turning orange, fading as the sun went down, people in shorts and backpacks milling around. Frank Chang stepped off the train with them. He stayed with the pack as they moved through the gate and onto the Ravinia grounds. When they were through the gate, he filtered off on his own and walked toward the pavilion.

To his left was the café and the meadow beyond. People on blankets and lawn chairs, drinking wine and taking food out of their picnic baskets. Children playing in the carousel. Frank could hear the music now. Classical music coming from a symphony, but it was alien to him. He had not been educated, not been taught to appreciate such things. Nor had he any exposure to it. He did not recognize the melody, but he could read the signs, which said, "Sunday in the Park with Mozart."

Frank looked to his right. Another meadow. Frank let his gaze rest there and then move beyond. He was supposed to be waiting here.

Fuck.

There was Sik-ho, wearing jeans and a T-shirt and a sportcoat, talking with a fucking girl. Smiling, animated . . . *flirting.* The goddamn fool. Sik-ho of Vancouver, British Columbia, chatting up a girl who could well remember his face.

Frank thought, where do they get these guys? It was one of the problems with *guanxi.* The Chinese philosophy that doesn't quite have an English equivalent definition. Basically, it meant connection. Network. Sik-ho had doubtless been recommended by someone Wong had respected. Or knew. Which was fine, if it worked out. But if the man was a fool and an amateur, Frank Chang would still have to work with him. Sik-ho was young, perhaps in his mid-twenties. Lusting for white girls. Or maybe he was bored. But they were here to do a job, not get fucked.

I should've known, Frank thought. Should have known by Sik-ho's body language that he was going to be difficult. Leaning against the wall when the deputy master came into the room. Risking face before the job had even begun. It was a bad omen then. Now it was worse. Had Frank not been otherwise acculturated, he would have canceled the whole thing right now. Got back in touch with Wong's man and told him that he needed to work with professionals, not punks.

But he was not in a position to make such a demand and he knew it. They had selected these men along with him and they had put him in charge. He was the Red Pole, they were the 49s. If he questioned that, he would not only risk face to Wong, he would risk it to his own *shan chu* in New York. If there were problems in the field, he was supposed to be able to handle them.

Frank moved closer to the meadow, willing Sik-ho to look up and catch his stare. Sik-ho eventually did, and Frank thought, *if he waves at me, I'll kill him.*

But Sik-ho didn't. He talked with the girl for a couple more moments and then came over to Frank.

Sik-ho said in English, "What's up?"

Frank said, "Making friends?"

"We were just talking."

"Did you give her your number and address in Vancouver?"

"Come on, I'm not stupid. She thinks my name is Peter."

"What if she remembers you?"

"She won't. I'm just another Chink." Sik-ho was smiling now, being funny.

Frank Chang sighed, willing his anger to go away. He said, "Where is he?"

Sik-ho pointed toward the pavilion. "He's in there. His two men are with him."

"They still there?"

"Yes."

"You sure?"

"Yeah. Look, I've been paying attention."

Frank said, "There will be an intermission in approximately twenty minutes. He may leave then. The second act is long and he may not want to stay for it. Either way, we wait for him."

"Okay."

Frank pointed to the café. "You wait there. Don't befriend any more women."

Sik-ho hesitated. Frank gave him a mild stare, waiting for him to say something smart or make some other move. But it passed.

Sik-ho said, "You're the boss."

DEA Agent Glenn Koshansky had told his supervisor that he thought this would be a waste of time. He didn't think Robert Wo was likely to spend his Sunday driving out to his lab refining heroin. He said this partly because he believed it. But he also said it because he didn't want to spend his Sunday working. His sup had said, "But it's over-time."

Which was true, but higher up in the chain of command they threw shit-fits about overtime. Glenn knew a guy who had worked a day's overtime without prior authorization and they docked him a day's pay just to clear the books. Cheap shit, even for management; using discipline to keep things evened out at payroll, but they'd done it anyway.

Was it worth messing with because of

Robert Wo?

Well, maybe. If the guy was actually the heroin expert they thought he was. But even if that were true, it wouldn't bring them any closer to the supposed chemist's secret chocolate factory. The Chinese were so secretive and if you were lucky enough to find one of their labs and smack it down, another one would just pop up somewhere else. It was like playing whack-a-mole.

The guy was here to listen to the symphony, for Christ's sake. He'd listen to the interminable strains of classical music, get into his Mercedes-Benz with his bodyguards, and then drive to his home in Evanston. A whole night's work for nothing and then they'd blame the agent for wasting DEA overtime on a nothing mission.

Agent Koshansky wondered what their reaction would be if he had paid the sixty bucks for a seat in the pavilion. *You what?* But he hadn't. He'd sit out here on the green grass with all the glorified bums and snotty turds with their wine and their bookbags and their bogus intellectual conversation. May as well be on a fucking commune.

Koshansky looked again at the symphony program. The first act would be ending soon and there would be an intermission. If God was smiling on him, Wo would decide to leave and Koshansky could get home in time to see the Sunday night sports wrap-up on ESPN.

The symphony topped off the first act with the "Clarinet Concerto KV 622." Wo had been looking forward to this, having seen it in the program, and when it came he enjoyed it as he would have an unexpected gift. The movement, the flow, the crescendo. Perfect. They had played the "Turkish March" too, though their pianist had not been as good as the one he had seen in New York six years earlier.

The concerto concluded, the conductor took his bow, and the orchestra left the stage. Wo walked to the café, his two bodyguards going with him. They sipped orangeades and bottled water for twelve minutes and returned to the pavilion for the second act.

But after a couple of pieces, Wo became restless. They had dropped Mozart and were now doing John Williams pieces. "Celebrating the Movies." Themes from *Superman, Raiders of the Lost Ark,* etc. The audience enjoying it, unfortunately . . . the symphony did these things occasionally to appeal to the masses. Well done, Wo supposed, but it was hard to give emotional investment to such works. They were recognizable melodies to be sure, but they were written for the screen, not the ear.

Wo signaled to his men. They moved out of the pavilion and toward the exit gates and the parking lot beyond.

When he saw them leave the pavilion, Glenn Koshansky breathed a sigh of relief. He picked them up near the Martin Theatre and kept about forty yards behind them as they walked to the parking lot. Wo was going home and after he did, Agent Koshansky would call it a night as well. Another night wasted. That was the thing about these criminal subjects, particularly ones allegedly involved in drug trafficking. You ended up working their hours. They set the agenda, not you. He remembered that scene in the gangster movie where De Niro raps on the window of the car of the feds that were tailing him. "Wake up, fuckos," he says. Telling them they needed to be on their toes if they were going to be following him. Taunting them. Well, maybe the feds had got tired of hiding.

But Koshansky was reasonably sure that neither Wo nor his men knew about him. Though he doubted they would change much if they did. A paid government watcher, having to bicker about overtime.

Koshansky saw them get into a white late-model Mercedes, Wo getting in the back with one of the guards, the other one getting behind the wheel.

Koshansky slowed, then stopped.

Watched as the taillights came on, then the reverse lights going white as the Mercedes started backing up.

A yellow cab came from the right, not going too fast, but not too slow anyway and Koshansky thought the cab would decelerate now because the Mercedes was blocking it.

But that's not what happened. The cab seemed to hesitate and then accelerated, picking up speed and smacking the Mercedes in the rear.

The cabbie got out. He was an almost slight man, wearing a White Sox ball cap. He shook his head at what he'd done and came to the front of the cab, as the driver of the Mercedes got out to check the damage.

The driver of the Mercedes was walking down the length of the car when Koshansky saw a motion behind the driver, an arm raised —

"Oh, shit," Koshansky said.

And heard the telltale pops, three of them,

88

and saw the driver of the Mercedes fall forward, the man behind him now fully visible, holding a .22 pistol. He had shot the driver in the back of the head, a professional hit.

Koshansky reached for his gun and as he was doing it, he saw the back door of the Mercedes flip open and the cabbie got behind the trunk of the Mercedes as the second bodyguard put his attention on the assassin on the other side and in doing so took his attention off the cab and the third man getting out of the rear of the cab and leveling a machine gun at him and pulling the trigger.

The second bodyguard went down. Koshansky was in the open, but he had drawn his weapon and had called out, "Halt!" Saw the cabbie crouched down looking at him with surprise, but there were two more, the one on the driver's side pointing the .22 at him, but hesitating and Koshansky turned and realized he'd made a rookie mistake, the assassin by the driver's side calling out "no" as the machine gunner fired on Koshansky. Koshansky returned fire, once, twice, three times before he went down.

Frank Chang saw the man go to the ground, then opened the driver's door. He saw Wo in the corner crouched down. He was not armed. He made eye contact briefly with Chang and Chang shot him twice in the head and once in the chest. Chang came out of the car. He made a gesture to Sik-ho and Sik-ho got back in the cab. Frank got in the back with him. Yu-shi got back behind the wheel and they left.

They cleared the parking lot of the Festival. The plan was to get to the parking lot of a Glencoe mall and take different vehicles from there. Yu-shi was a good driver and he would feel better once they had merged in with interstate traffic.

Sik-ho said to Frank, "Did you get him?"

"Yeah, I got him."

Sik-ho was laughing now. The machine gun was on the floorboard. Frank wanted to hit him, the crazy fuck. Killing a man that was almost certainly a policeman. He could wait till they got to Glencoe and then dress him down. Or just hit him now, wipe that stupid smile off his face. Laughing for some reason.

"Oh, no," Frank said.

Sik-ho was bleeding on his right shoulder. He'd been hit.

Sik-ho said, "Don't worry, boss man. It's just a wound. That cop was fucking stupid. He should have stayed out of it."

"You're a fool," Frank said. "You know we're not supposed to involve outsiders."

"He should have stayed out of it."

"And what about you? Are we supposed to take you to a hospital now?"

Upfront, Yu-shi said, "No. We're not taking him to any hospital."

"Who the fuck asked you?" Sik-ho said.

"We'll take you back to Wong's," Yu-shi said, "but no hospital."

"Who said I want to go to a hospital?" Sik-ho said. "I told you *dil-nay,* it's just a wound."

Frank looked in the rearview mirror. He was seeking Yu-shi's expression there and Yu-shi gave it to him and Frank knew they were both thinking the same thing. A shot to the arm, but bleeding profusely. Were that the case, they'd have to get him to a hospital within twenty minutes, tops. And in that quick moment of eye contact, they both knew that they were not even going to try.

NINE

Preston Wong asked, "Where is he now?"

"He's in the trunk," Frank said.

They had switched out the cab with a secondhand Lexus in Glencoe. Sik-ho had bled out by the time they got there. But Frank didn't want to leave him in the cab. Partly because it wouldn't be a good idea to leave a dead man in the parking lot of a mall, partly because of the Chinese respect for the dead. Funerals are important to the Chinese.

Frank Chang had not liked Sik-ho, but that was beside the point.

Now they were back at Wong's warehouse in Chinatown. Frank had told Hsu-shen what had happened, all of it, and Hsu-shen had called Wong away from a family dinner.

Wong said, "The other man is dead too?"

"I think so."

"And you think he was a policeman?"

"I believe he was. He was not in uniform,

but the way he carried himself and called out halt . . . I would say he was police."

Hsu-shen said, "Did you know he was there?"

Frank said, "No. Not until then."

"Shouldn't you have?"

"I don't know," Frank said. "Perhaps."

Wong said, "And you think he's dead? The policeman, that is?"

"Yes."

Hsu-shen smiled and said, "Does that bother you, Red-Pole?"

Frank Chang said, "Yes. I didn't kill him."

Wong said, "But you were in charge. You're responsible."

"I suppose I am, Mister Wong. But I didn't pick Sik-ho," Frank said. "I would not have either."

Hsu-shen turned on Frank with a sharp look. "Are you questioning Mister Wong?"

"No. I'm only saying that Sik-ho was too young and inexperienced for this. He should have left the policeman alone."

Hsu-shen said, "He was under your supervision."

"And I told him not to shoot the policeman."

Yu-shi had been quiet up till then, though he had been listening to all of it. Now he spoke, saying, "It happened so quickly."

"Forget about it," Wong said. "It's passed. Fortunately, the policeman is dead. He can't identify either of you. Besides, it was a matter between us. He should have kept out of it."

Us, Frank Chang thought. The Chinese gangsters. Kill each other, but try to leave outsiders out of it. Not because they thought the white devils were a superior race and did not deserve to die. It certainly wasn't that. It was just bad business. Little yellow people shooting each other and little yellow witnesses thereafter saying they didn't see or hear anything. What could the white police do in the face of that, other than to throw up their hands and say, "There's no helping these people. They won't help themselves." But when outsiders, non–gang members, got involved, that was when the Americans came crashing down like a hammer. It had happened in San Francisco years ago. One gang involved in a turf war with another, sending assassins to a restaurant in Chinatown with machine guns. They went in without proper planning, blazing away like maniacs. Several customers were killed and not one of them was a member of the rival gang. "Innocent bystanders," and that was all they got. One of them was a Japanese law student, no more a gangster than your grandmother. Innocent bystanders murdered and that was what brought the police into Chinatown and, for a while, shut down the San Francisco triads. It was what happened when you didn't use professionals to do the job.

This was not Frank Chang's town. For now, he was under the command of Preston Wong. It was not his place to second guess their decisions. But he wanted them to know he would not have picked Sik-ho. An American policeman was dead now and they would not forget about that.

Hsu-shen was eyeing Frank again, thinking of something he could say that would cut, and Frank was not surprised when he did.

Hsu-shen said, "Do you want to leave now, Chang?"

Frank thought that maybe they would let him leave. Get on a train or plane for New York, though he would prefer a train. But even if they let him go, it would cost him immense face. And not just for him, but for his own triad in New York as well. He would be finished.

Frank said, "No. You brought me here for two jobs. I've still one left. If after that, you don't want to pay me, I won't object."

Wong looked from Hsu-shen to Frank

Chang. For now Wong's own face was at stake, if he openly welched on an agreement. Or was thought to.

Wong said, "You'll be paid, as we agreed." Wong was aware of the man from Hong Kong as well, but did not make eye contact with him when he added, "As will Yu-shi and Sik-ho's family."

Wong made a gesture to his own second, Hsu-shen. They spoke briefly and Wong walked away.

Hsu-shen said to Frank and Yu-shi, "Get some rest. You will finish the job tomorrow. Then you'll be paid and leave town."

Hsu-shen walked out to Wong's car with him. Then they were standing by Wong's Jaguar, the street dark and cool, in the distance the sound of the elevated train going from north to south.

Hsu-shen said, "Do you want me to take this over?"

"I've thought about that," Wong said. "But we brought these men in for a reason. It is the way these things are done."

"If they know what they're doing," Hsu-shen said.

"They did it," Wong said. "Wo is dead and that is what we wanted. Tomorrow, Liu and then they're gone. You are concerned?"

"About the policeman?"

"Yes."

"No. He should not have been there," Hsu-shen said. "What worries me is Chang."

"Because he's concerned? About the policeman?"

"Because he hesitated. That is from his own mouth, Preston. He hesitated to kill the policeman. Sik-ho did not."

Preston Wong gave this some thought. He was experienced at hiding his emotions, and drew on that experience now to hide his anger at Frank Chang. There was something superior about the man that got under Wong's skin. Offering to forgo payment. It had been a clever insult. He had wanted to take Chang aside then and say something hard to him, let him know that he was under his command now. Tell him he was not in New York and that he was not a *shan chu* in the Wu-Chai or the White Lotus. Chang was a mid-level officer and nothing more. But to speak to Chang like that in front of the others would have cost Wong face.

Now Wong said, "He is of the White Lotus." Meaning, that killing him could have consequences.

Hsu-shen said, "Perhaps he is getting old. Tired. Would they miss a warrior who hesitates to protect himself? Who hesitates to protect his own?"

"Maybe not," Wong said.

TEN

Maitland saw it on the ten o'clock news. An agent for the Drug Enforcement Agency shot and killed at Ravinia's. He thought of his friend Jay Jackson, a DEA agent himself. His heart stopping for a moment and then the anchor said the agent's name and Maitland realized it wasn't Jay, but someone he didn't know. They said the agent was thirty years old and had a wife and a baby.

Shit, Maitland thought. Young guy who probably never saw it coming. And why would he? Ravinia's? The anchor went to the on-location reporter, a young lady of earnest good looks. She said the police had no witnesses at this time, which was something of a surprise with Sunday night crowds.

And Maitland thought, no, not really. Killers can hide in crowds. Slip away while people are still screaming in panic, indeed, actually *hoping* that the killer has left.

Maitland was in his apartment alone when he saw this. Julie had telephoned earlier to say that she was tired and had family things and would not be spending the night with him. Maitland said that was fine, his voice polite and easy. Sometimes it was better not to ask.

But he picked up the phone now and called her. She answered and said, "Hey."

"Hi," Maitland said. "Did you see the news?"

Julie said, "The shooting?"

"Yeah."

"Yes. Terrible."

Maitland said, "Did you know him?"

"No. I never worked anything with DEA. Didn't you, back in the day?" Referring to Maitland's undercover narcotics work.

Maitland said, "Yeah. That's how I know Jay Jackson. But I never met this guy. Or heard of him."

After a moment, Julie said, "It's Highland Park's jurisdiction. But it'll be a federal case because of him."

Maitland said, "Well . . . I just wanted to call to see if you were okay."

"I understand," Julie said.

She did too. Maitland was not the sort to think she couldn't handle herself. He had not called because he suspected she would be sobbing uncontrollably. Nor had he really thought that she knew the DEA agent. The bottom line was, the DEA agent and Julie Ciskowski were part of the greater law enforcement community of the Chicago area. Because the man had died in the line of duty, there would be a funeral and police from all over Chicago would attend, be they metro, state, or federal. It was their way. Chicago detective Julie Ciskowski was part of that community.

Evan Maitland was not. Not anymore, and he knew it. He could attend the funeral, but people would think he was out of place. Unwelcome. He would think it himself. He was not a cop anymore. Nor was he retired cop. He had resigned under pressure and that was the difference. His innocence was beside the point.

Julie said, "I appreciate you calling."

"Okay."

"I'll . . . be in touch with you soon."

"Okay. Goodnight, Julie."

"Goodnight, Evan."

Maitland hung up the phone.

Silence. He had turned the television off when Julie answered the telephone. He left it off now and contemplated things.

Julie.

· Maybe she was moving out, maybe breaking it off with him. If so, doing it indirectly. Or maybe she was just thinking about it. Or maybe she just needed time alone to think. She was a tough lady and not one given to melodrama.

As for tonight, he wasn't quite sure why he had called her. It was not his intention to ask her to come over. Certainly, it would have been stupid to say something like, "come back." Because she hadn't really left. Time and a place for that sort of conversation. The murder of the DEA agent had triggered something. A concern for a fellow officer. If she had known him, she'd probably want to discuss it with someone. She had left her husband — for good reason — about a year ago. She had no children. Her relationship with her parents was okay, but it was not one of particular closeness. This was partly because her parents disapproved of some of the choices she had made in her life — joining the police department, staying there, divorcing her asshole of a husband, not having children. Maitland thought it might also include getting involved with an antiques dealer who demonstrated no real signs of long-term commitment. In short, she had not turned out to be the sort of person they wanted their little girl to be.

Maitland also knew she had difficulty

making friends at the police department. A lot of the men wanted to sleep with her. Or if they didn't, they wanted to sort of make her a daughter figure, taking orders and guidance from papa bear, and they'd resent her if she showed a reasonable disinclination to this role. Her last supervising captain had been one of these breed. When she divorced, a lot of them thought it would be open season, as she said. And they were not happy to learn that she had taken up with Maitland, the ex-cop.

If you're tough and independent and you know yourself pretty well, it shouldn't matter to you too much what others think. But Maitland knew that at a police department, it did matter. He knew from personal experience what it was to go to work and feel like you don't have one friend. It was the way he felt after he had been cleared of the corruption charge and the administrative investigation. He won and was legally allowed to keep his job. But that was on paper. He returned to a department of averted glances and conversations coming to a halt when he walked up. It didn't matter that he was innocent. The mob had turned against him.

He had never quite figured out why. Perhaps it was because Terry Specht, the internal affairs investigator, had persuaded the rest of the department that Maitland was guilty and had only escaped punishment because of a clever union lawyer. Or perhaps it was because he had worked undercover for so long, had taken on the appearance of the turd drug dealer, that the uniforms couldn't really tell the difference. Maybe to them, he was a turd too. Even though they were the ones that had assigned him to narcotics in the first place.

Or maybe they didn't need a reason. Maybe this was how mob action worked. *There's the guy! Let's get him!* Even though it's the wrong guy. It's not the truth that matters, but the emotion of the moment.

Maitland tried to avoid self-pity. He knew in some ways that he was a lucky man. But even today a certain memory could get under his skin: Melvin Monroe. One of the old guard. A big man with a bad temper who should have never been a cop, but whose type often is. Melvin's wife was one of the photographers at the city booking station. One day a punk was arrested and brought in for fingerprints and photos. The punk, being funny, said to Mrs. Monroe, "Why don't you take another picture for yourself? You can take it to bed with you tonight." Mrs. Monroe did not take another picture. But she did tell Melvin about it. Melvin went straight to the punk's cell, ordered it open, and went to work on him. They had to carry the punk out on a stretcher, his arm broken and contusions to his head.

There was an administrative investigation. Also conducted by Terry Specht. At the end of it, Terry recommended that a letter of reprimand be given to Melvin Monroe. The letter remained in Melvin's file for six months and was then removed. There was no termination, no demotion, no suspension without pay, no criminal investigation. The thing was, people *liked* Melvin. When he was cleared, people clapped him on the shoulder and welcomed him back. This reception was not repeated for Maitland when he was investigated that same year . . . *Ah, Don Corleone, why was Melvin so liked and I so hated? . . .* When Maitland thought about things like this, he wondered if he was better off being run out of there.

"Shit," Maitland said, angry at himself for giving it this much thought. He stood up and walked to the kitchen to get a beer. It was years ago and it was silly to dwell on it now. He was alive, and some poor kid with the DEA was dead.

As for Julie, she was a grown woman. If

she wanted to stay with the PD, it would be up to her.

ELEVEN

Bianca said, "You sold this?"

She was pointing to a Louis XV armoire. Solid carved walnut, from the Rhone Valley.

"Yeah," Maitland said.

"When?"

"Linda Cahn. She called me on my cell phone this morning."

"Oh," Bianca said. "She was here Wednesday, wasn't she?"

"Yeah."

"She paid the asking price?"

"Every bit."

They were at their store. Colette's Antiques, it was called, though neither one of them went by that name. They stuck mainly to French and Italian pieces, though they would not turn down a valuable treasure if they saw it.

Bianca said, "Has she got room for it?" Linda Cahn had bought a lot of things from them already. She had money and she liked to spend it.

Maitland shrugged. "Maybe she wants a place for her children's toys."

Bianca said, "Have you been to her home?"

"I don't think so."

"I have. It's a little sad, really. She has no . . . sense of where to put things. It's cluttered."

"You tell her that?"

"Oh, no."

"Recommend an interior decorator to her."

"She's got one. Tracy Inman."

"Oh . . . yeah."

"That's how I feel. You know, Tracy's basically a crook. Stupid too. She takes women like Linda who have no sense of style and no culture and just gets them to spend all their money. Then bills her a fortune for her 'time.' And then her house just looks tacky."

Maitland said, "It makes her happy."

"It doesn't make her happy, Evan. It just makes her feel less lonely. Tracy pretends to be this poor woman's friend."

"You want to do an intervention?"

"Oh, shut up. No, I'm not gonna interfere."

"You just want to complain to me about it."

"Yes."

"Bianca?"

"Yes?"

"What makes me or you any different from Tracy Inman?"

"Come on, Evan. You sold Linda a quality antique. Something she can give to her children, something that is historic."

"It's furniture."

"It's not furniture, you bastard. Besides, you don't believe that anyway. You just want to irritate me."

"Yeah, sort of."

"Besides, we're not getting additional money from Linda just to go to the fuckin' Pottery Barn with her."

"Such language from a lady."

"We're selling something of value."

"To a woman with money. Who's bored and feels better when she spends it."

"That doesn't mean it's okay to exploit her."

"No, it's not."

"What do you think of John Roseland?"

"John . . . gay guy?"

"Yeah. Interior decorator."

"He's all right. He's a good decorator. Nice guy, too."

"We should steer Linda to him. He's honest and he's got a good eye."

"Aww, I don't want to get involved in something like that. Tracy finds out about it, she'll call up here threatening to sue us."

"For what?"

"There doesn't have to be anything to it. She'll give us heat anyway for costing her a customer."

"I don't care if she does. She's a bitch anyway."

"Well, at least be subtle about it."

"I'm always subtle," Bianca said.

"Yeah," Maitland said. "Always."

"I'm not gonna talk to you no more."

"Hmmm," Maitland said.

Bianca stood up. She said, "Do you want some coffee?"

"Yeah, if you're getting some."

Bianca took his cup from his desk. She poured out what was left into the kitchen sink. Poured enough milk to cover the bottom of the cup, then poured coffee on top of that. She brought it back to his desk and set it in front of him.

Maitland thanked her and said, "So how was the party?"

"It was okay. I met this Chinese dealer. I think he can help us find that chicken cup Lana Wilmarth wanted."

"The Cheng-gu —"

"The Cheng*hua* chicken cups."

"He's got one?"

"He thinks he can get one."

"Who is this?"

"Raymond Liu," Bianca said. "I've heard of him before, but I'd never met him. He's supposed to call sometime today."

"That's great news, Bianca."

"We'll see," she said. "So. You went to Cleveland?"

"Yes."

"Shoot up the place?"

"No. It was very peaceful. I won some money."

"Money? You go to a casino?"

"No. It was a card game." He wanted to tell her about it, describing the hands and the flop and the betting strategies. He said, "You ever play Texas hold-em'?"

"Texas what?"

"Texas . . . oh, never mind."

The telephone rang about forty minutes before noon. Maitland answered it.

"Colette's Antiques."

"Hello. May I speak to Bianca, please?"

"Who's calling?"

"Raymond Liu."

"Hold on a minute."

Bianca took the phone a few seconds later. She was aware in her way and she expected that Liu would ask her out to lunch. She would be okay with that, give him signals that lunch would be for business purposes only, but she was surprised when he told her he had some photos of some pieces that were available in Seattle and could she come by his apartment this evening to examine them?

Bianca said, "I suppose I could. Are you not able to do it earlier?"

"I'm afraid not. I have appointments all day, and this evening is one of the few free ones I have."

"Okay," Bianca said.

"My apartment is in Hyde Park. Shall we say eight-thirty?"

"Okay," Bianca said. "Tell me your address."

It turned out not to be an apartment in an apartment building, but an apartment on the second floor of a large house. A duplex that had been fashioned from a home built in the early part of the twentieth century. Bianca parked her car on the street and walked to the front porch. Dark and quiet out. She rang the doorbell.

The light came on inside, illuminating a stairway going up to the second floor. And then there was Raymond Liu, standing at the top of the stairs, waving at her before he came down. He was smiling as he descended the stairs and Bianca didn't like that smile.

There are women who make a point of turning down a man's advance gracefully and there are women who are aware that some men wouldn't take a cue even if you broke one over their heads. Bianca had been married for over ten years and in that time she had never been unfaithful to her husband. That is, she had not had sexual relations with another man. Certainly, she was no nun. She was aware of men who were attractive and was aware of being attractive to men. However, in her way, she sometimes felt she had strayed. It was when she was in a motel bed with Evan. Nothing had happened; he was recovering from a gunshot wound, his body learning to adjust to having one less lung. Maitland was asleep and needing to be. But Bianca had laid next to him. Not touching, not kissing, not making love. But an intimacy had been acknowledged then. At least by her. She and Maitland had never discussed it.

She never told Max about this. She saw no need to. Max trusted her and he was not by nature an inquisitor. He had his life and his career and she had hers.

But she was a beautiful woman, exotic and

rare to many Americans. So there had been invitations to dinners and shows. And once in a while a man would rest a hand on her arm or leg, waiting for a signal that it was okay to proceed. She would shift her body so their hand would fall or, if that didn't work, simply pick their hand up and set it away from her. It usually worked. Though once or twice she had to say, "What are you doing?", her voice sharp.

As Raymond Liu opened the door, she thought it was fifty-fifty at best that he had done any research on the Chenghua chicken cups. Liu seemed like a bit of a clumsy man, not a Warren Beatty–type womanizer, but more of an oaf. They could be worse than the other. Unattractive, nerdy types who had never had much luck with girls, but with time and success and money, come to feel they're entitled.

Liu opened the door and said, "I'm glad you could come." He said it like it was a date.

Bianca said, "No problem. I have to warn you, though, I don't have much time."

"Of course. Come on up."

He led her up the stairs into a modestly furnished apartment. There were a couple of Chinese artifacts spread about and some books on the shelf. For show, Bianca thought. He doesn't live here. It's set up for such a rendezvous. A love nest.

Before she could speak, Liu said, "Would you like some wine?"

Shit.

Bianca said, "Mr. Liu, I don't mean to be impolite, but you do have photos of the chicken cups, don't you?"

"Of course. They're over there on the table."

Bianca looked over. There were indeed photos spread about on a table.

"Okay," she said, "I just don't want to give you the wrong impression."

"About what?"

Jesus.

"About me," she said. "I'm married and I'm not interested in having an affair. If that's all you're interested in, I'm leaving. If you want to actually do business with me, we'll both forget about this and move on. I leave it to you. Okay?" She did not scold or judge when she said this, but rather spoke plainly. Experience had taught her that was usually the best way.

Liu hadn't been ready for it. Not so early, anyway. Now he was processing it, as they stood a reasonable distance apart.

If he had said something like, "Are you sure?" she would have left. If he had moved toward her for a kiss, she would have shoved him off and left. Maybe hit him in the head with her cell phone if that didn't work.

But he didn't. He just smiled and said, "Okay. Forgive me for behaving badly."

"It's okay. You're a man. Are those legitimate photos?"

"As a matter of fact, they are. Would you like some coffee while we go over them?"

"That sounds great."

Hsu-shen said, "I'm coming with you."

Frank Chang regarded him for a moment, then said, "Why?"

"You'll need three. You, myself, and Yu-shi."

"We won't need three. Liu has no bodyguards."

"He's probably expecting you now. After what happened last night."

"Yu-shi's been studying him since this morning. There are no bodyguards."

"Did you see this?"

"Yu-shi did."

Hsu-shen said, "That's not the same. We don't want another mistake."

Frank said, "You relieving me of command?"

"Yes. Your rank means nothing here."

"That's not what Wong said when I got here."

"That was before you bungled the job."

They were in the warehouse, standing near the Lexus that would take them to Liu's home. Yu-shi stood nearby, keeping quiet.

Frank Chang took the insult, kept his temper. He said, "If he's unhappy, he can send us home."

Hsu-shen said, "You're not finished yet. You can leave when you are."

"If that is how it is, then I'm still in charge."

"Are you refusing to take orders from me?"

"Yes."

They were standing a distance apart. Frank was armed, a .45 pistol in his belt. Hsu-shen was wearing a jacket and who knew if he had a gun in it or not. But Frank was aware of Hsu-shen's expertise in martial arts. If he saw the beginning of a strike from a fist or foot, he would draw his weapon and shoot him. Yu-shi was aware of a stand-off now and he quietly stepped back.

Moments passed, the men staring at each other, and Frank could see that Hsu-shen was thinking it over. He could try to kill Frank and if he succeeded, he'd have to explain it to Wong later. Maybe that was what he was thinking . . . maybe he was thinking that he didn't care about the consequences.

Hsu-shen said, "These are Wong's orders."

"Then let him tell me," Frank said. "Until then, I'm the Red Pole."

Hsu-shen stared at him for a little while. Then he gave a tight smile. "Have it your way," he said. "But I'm still coming."

"No one said you couldn't," Frank said.

They picked him up at his office. Watched him come out and get into a Range Rover and drive south on Lake Shore, continuing past Grant Park, and Frank knew he was going to his private apartment in Hyde Park intead of to his house in Oak Park.

Frank was sitting up front, with Yu-shi driving. Hsu-shen was in the backseat. Frank put his back in the corner, set so that he could see if Hsu-shen was going to try to reach for a gun and shoot him in the back of the head. He wanted this thing to be finished so he could get back to New York. Frank had taken oaths for his triad, not Preston Wong's. One of those oaths was that he would never betray his sworn brothers. To do so was to risk being killed by the myriad of swords. Literally. Frank had seen it done, men getting up to a hundred cuts on their back until they bleed to death. Hsu-shen was not his brother, but he could see madness and violence in Hsu-shen's eyes. Hsu-shen was looking for an excuse to kill him. Maybe waiting for an opportunity. That was one of the problems when triads shared labor. Personalities rubbed against each other and there was no oath to protect you from another triad. There was no "we're all Chinese" mentality. Not even close. He was here at the request of the Wu-Chai Triad to inflict harm on the Red Lantern Triad. A mercenary who may or may not be dispensable. A Chinese brought in by Chinese to kill other Chinese.

This was not the sort of thing to fill Frank Chang with doubt or self-introspection. But he had survived these years by trusting his instincts. And that instinct was telling him that his own life was increasingly in danger the longer he remained in this city.

Frank said, "There it is." He pointed and said to Yu-shi, "Keep going. Don't park in front of it. Park around the corner."

Yu-shi drove the car around the corner and parked in front of a white house. Frank looked out the window and saw a crew of men working in a yard across the street. There were three men, Hispanic or black, and they were loading landscaping equipment into the back of a trailer hitched to a pickup.

"Wait," Frank said.

Hsu-shen said, "Let's go."

"No," Frank said, motioning with his head to the men across the street. Witnesses. "We can't park here. They've seen us."

Hsu-shen smiled and said, "You think they're policemen? They're workmen. Nobodies."

Frank spoke to Yu-shi as if Hsu-shen was not there. "Start the car," Frank said. "Take us away. Come back in fifteen minutes."

"No," Hsu-shen said.

"Do it," Frank said.

"It isn't necessary," Hsu-shen said.

"They're finishing the job," Frank said. "We'll come back later. They won't be here then. Liu will." Frank turned and gave Hsu-shen a look, putting him in his place. Then he turned to Yu-shi and said, "Go on." The thing was decided.

Yu-shi started the car.

They came back fifteen minutes later. The landscaping crew was gone.

After Yu-shi had parked the car, Frank said to him, "He lives on the second floor. Go around the back and go up the back stairs. I'll sneak up the front. If he tries to go out

120

the back, take him."

Frank spoke as if Hsu-shen was not in the car. It was intended. He did not turn around to see Hsu-shen's glare.

Frank walked down the street, the house up on his right coming closer into view. He looked up and saw yellow light coming through the top windows. It meant that Liu was there. Hopefully not someone else. Frank kept his eyes on the windows, the lights off below, no one home there. He did not see anybody peering out the top windows and he walked up the steps, quietly, and put himself in front of the door.

The light was off in the stairway. That was good. Frank tried the doorknob. Locked. It was an old house. Frank was in the shadows now on the porch. He took the .45 from his jacket pocket and screwed a silencer on the top. He did that before he used a slim piece of steel to force the door open. This worked and then he stepped inside the stairwell and closed the door behind him.

He began moving up the stairs.

Hsu-shen followed Yu-shi down the alley. He did not try to hide it. At one point, Yu-shi turned and looked at him. Hsu-shen nodded and Yu-shi kept going. When Yu-shi reached the duplex, Hsu-shen stepped into some trees and put himself behind a trash dumpster.

Frank Chang reached the top of the stairs. He turned the corner to see a door that was opened. He heard movement, a man breathing, walking. Frank came into the front room. There was no one there. Frank walked out and saw the man standing in what would be the dining room. Standing and looking down at photos on a table.

Frank said, "Raymond?"

The man answered with his eyes. Frank raised the pistol and fired three times. The shots threw Raymond Liu back and he knocked over a chair when he went down. Frank walked over and put another bullet in his forehead.

The shot to the head had not been necessary. Raymond Liu was already dead.

Frank Chang turned around.

There was a woman in the corner, standing next to a telephone stand. She was looking at him, her expression wide with horror. A white woman with her mouth open.

Frank said, "What are you doing here?"

She didn't answer him. She simply stared back at him.

And then her stare shifted to the doorway to the kitchen behind.

Yu-shi standing there, his gun at his side. He looked at the woman for only a second then turned and fired at Frank, the bullet hitting him in the chest. It knocked him back against the wall. Frank went to the ground and looked up as Yu-shi walked around the table to shoot him again and Frank raised his gun and shot Yu-shi in the face. That was the end of him.

Frank sat up and scooted back to the wall. He remained in a seated position. He looked over at the woman. She was still in the corner, not screaming. She was probably in shock. But she was looking at him now, perhaps waiting for it.

Frank shook his head. He motioned with his chin toward the back of the house.

"Get out of here," he said. "Go through the back. *Go.*"

TWELVE

In war, they say you never hear the shell that hits you. It just hits and then you're done. Or maybe you do hear it and yet your unconscious simply steps aside.

Bianca had never seen a man get shot before. Had never seen what bullets do to people. She had never seen what a .45 pistol would do to a man's face. It was all too fast. Like standing in a room and then the floor's gone and you fall through to the next level. No whine indicating an incoming rocket. Just motion and then it's over.

She had been standing in the corner to use the telephone. She had picked up the phone to call Max and tell him where she was and that she should be home in forty-five minutes. She was going to say that she should have called sooner, but she forgot. They had not planned dinner, but he would worry after eight o'clock. She had not dialed a number yet when the Chinese man walked into the room and killed Raymond Liu.

When he turned and saw her, she did not have the breath to scream. She was immobile. She had heard muffled sounds — *phhht, phhht* — and she had seen Raymond go down and then saw that the Chinese man had a gun with something long stuck on the end of it. The Chinese man looking at her surprised and she thought, *No.* No, please. Please don't kill me. Entirely at his mercy, paralyzed with fear, an object to be discarded at his will. *Please.*

Still looking at him when the other man appeared in the kitchen doorway. Another Chinese man looking, then shooting the first one in the chest. That one on the ground pointing up and shooting the second one in the face and killing him.

Then the one on the ground saying, "Get out of here. Go through the back."

. . . on the ground and she had seen him fall, but he wasn't bleeding . . .

"Go."

Ordering her now and she moved and then she ran . . . through the kitchen and then down the back stairs. And perhaps she had misunderstood, perhaps he was kidnapping her, telling her she was going with him. Take her someplace else and when she got out the back door to see if he was behind her, holding his long gun and saying, "not too far" or just shooting her, but he wasn't there, she was alone and she walked through a small yard, fences on the sides, other houses with lights on, people watching television, it wasn't real, it couldn't be real, but she kept moving and then she was in the alleyway.

Remembering that her car was parked in front of Liu's house. Parked there and she would have to walk around to get it so she could get in and drive away from this nightmare, but she couldn't because the car was too close to the house, too close, and she needed to get away, get away, get far away from this place and call the police, dial 911 and tell them she had just seen two men shot to death, two Chinese-Americans, one of whom she knew, though not very well and Jesus Christ, he was dead now, shot to death in front of her very eyes. Get off this block, get away from this place, get your cell phone out and call 911 and get someplace safe . . . a diner, a theater, a bar . . . where the fuck were these things in a back alley in Hyde Park?

"Hey."

She turned around, slowing her walk, and surprised that she was walking and not running, maybe trying to avoid panic, maybe

126

panicking already, not thinking clearly and . . . the Chinese man had followed her, changed his mind, and was going to shoot her too.

"Hey. Come here."

He was about half a block behind her, standing in the middle of the alley. Dark out, but his clothes were lighter now.

"Come here," he said again.

And it didn't sound like him. It didn't sound like him because it wasn't him.

Bianca turned and ran.

"Hey!"

Hsu-shen went after her.

Bianca got to the end of the alley and turned to her right, away from the street where her car was parked. And it was still streets and apartments and homes, but no businesses, no lights, no comfort, and she kept going and as she reached the next corner she turned and looked behind her and the man was running for her, coming full speed, and she rounded the corner in time to see the bus pull away from the stop and she cried out, couldn't help it, crying out in a disappointment so hard it was almost physical, but kept going because up ahead were the blue and white signs of the Chicago Transit Authority, the turnstile doors, and the steps behind it, leading up to the elevated train and she ran, still hearing the steps behind her, and she pushed through the turnstile and went up the stairs, taking two at a time.

Hsu-shen saw her go up the stairs and seconds passed before he reached the stairs himself. Then he was through the turnstile and pounding up the stairs himself. And there was the train, the doors still open and the horn sounding off and he ran and got an arm in as the door closed, the door stopping then opening back up, and the train was moving and he got on and started moving through the cars.

The train roared off on the tracks and then the sound was in the distance and then it was gone.

Bianca got up from behind the end of the platform where she had been hiding. She climbed back onto the platform. It had been dirty down by the tracks, greasy too, and it had probably ruined her skirt. She walked back down the stairs and hailed a cab. Sighing to herself when one was there. *Where were you earlier, asshole?* She called the police once she was inside.

THIRTEEN

Her second call was to Maitland. He got to the south station of the police department after she did. They said she was being questioned by a couple of detectives and he could sit in the waiting room until they were finished. Maitland said he was her attorney and he needed to be there with her.

That put him in the interview room with her. One of the detectives had heard of Maitland before, knew someone who knew him, and said he could wait outside unless he had a bar card or some other proof that he was actually a lawyer, but Bianca said it didn't matter, she wanted him here anyway.

The detectives took it out on her by asking her to tell the story again. She started to, again, and the detective with the glasses held up a hand and said, "Now why were you meeting him there?" His name was Colyer.

Bianca said, "I told you before, he had

asked me to meet him there."

The detective with the mustache, whose name was Lundberg, said, "What for?"

"To go over photos of these Chinese antiques. My client was looking for a certain piece."

"Was there a special need to meet at his apartment?"

"I didn't think so. But he wanted to do it that way."

Detective Colyer said, "Mrs. Garibaldi, let me say something. I'm not your husband and I'm not here to judge you. But is there something you're not telling us?"

"Jesus Christ," Maitland said.

Bianca said, "No, there's nothing I'm not telling you. I was not having an affair with Mr. Liu. And I wasn't planning to either."

"You sure?"

"Yeah, I'm sure. What difference would it make anyway?"

Lundberg said, "We just want to find out what happened, ma'am. That's all."

"I told you what happened."

Colyer said, "Okay, we've got Mr. Liu, right? Then another Chinese guy coming up the front stairs. Bam, he shoots Liu. Then he points the gun at you."

"I don't . . . I don't remember that."

"You don't remember the Chinese guy —"

"I don't remember him pointing a gun at me. He seemed surprised that I was there."

"Could it be that he did and you forgot?"

Bianca said, "Now how am I supposed to answer that?"

"Okay. Then another guy comes in the back."

"He came in through the kitchen door."

"And he had a gun."

"Yes."

"Did he point it at you?"

"I . . . I'm not sure. He shot the other man."

"Liu?"

"No. He shot the one that shot Liu."

"The one that you say didn't point his gun at you?"

"Yes."

"You say the guy from the kitchen shot the guy that shot Liu?"

"Yes."

"And the guy that shot Liu shot the kitchen guy back?"

"Yes."

"And killed him?"

"Yes, I think so."

"And then what?"

"The man . . . the man that shot Raymond, he told me to go."

"He said go, with him?"

"No, just go. He said, 'Get out of here.' "

"Get out of here."

"Yes."

"Like, you were someplace you didn't belong?"

"Yes. Like that."

"And you went out the back?"

"Yes."

"And he followed you?"

"No. I mean, I thought he did at first. But it wasn't him. There was another man waiting in the alley. He was the one that chased me."

"And you say it was dark?"

"Yes."

"And you think he may have been Asian too."

"Yes."

"But you can't really give us much of a description beyond that?"

"No. I'm sorry."

"Then how do you know it wasn't the same guy? The same guy who shot Raymond Liu."

"I just know. The man who shot Raymond wore a dark jacket and a white shirt. The man in the alley was dressed differently."

"So," Detective Lundberg said, "you can remember clothes, but not much beyond that?"

Bianca gave him a look. "Yeah, I guess so."

Colyer said, "Mrs. Garibaldi —"

"It's Ms.," she said. "My husband's name is not Garibaldi."

"*Ms.* Garibaldi," he said. "We've got a problem. This second man you talked about, he's not at the apartment. We've got Mr. Liu and another man with his head more or less blown off. But there's no third man there." Colyer looked at her as he paused, looking for a reaction. "Can you explain that?"

Bianca shrugged. "He left."

Colyer said, "He left after he got shot?"

"I never said he had been killed. I told you. He was sitting on the floor after he shot the second man and he told me to get out of there."

"And then what," Lundberg said. "He just got up and walked out the front door?"

"I don't know where he went, sir. I didn't know the man."

Lundberg said, "But he knew you."

Maitland said, "No, he didn't."

Lundberg condescended to look over at him. "Excuse me?" he said, getting tough now.

Maitland said, "No, he didn't know her. She never told you that." He turned to Bianca. "Did you?"

"No. I didn't."

Lundberg said, "Was I talking to you?"

Maitland held up a hand. "Just trying to help," he said.

"Well, don't."

Maitland said, "Is this being recorded? I hope so, because I think a clear review of the record will show that she's given you zero indication that she knew this killer. The truth is, she has no idea why the man let her go. But I think it's obvious to anyone with any sense that he didn't go there to kill her."

Colyer said, "You through?"

Maitland said, "Yeah, for now."

Colyer said, "No one asked you to be here."

"She has. And she's under no obligation to cooperate with you in this investigation."

"She's a material witness. No one's arrested her."

Maitland said, "You just implied that she knew this fucking assassin. Now if you're going to pull shit like that, I'm going to advise her to plead the fifth and we'll come back here with a lawyer."

"Hold on —"

"For Christ's sake," Maitland said, "she's a *victim.* You sit here talking to her as if she's committed a crime."

"No, sir, we have —"

"Or that she was having an affair with this other man —"

"We have an investigation to conduct," Colyer said. "And who the hell are you to second guess us? With your record?"

"My record?" Maitland said. "Would you mind explaining that?"

Colyer said, "You know damn well what I'm talking about."

Maitland said, "I was cleared." He regretted saying it immediately. Defending himself to this idiot. Maitland said, "Who are you performing for, detective?"

"Fuck you." Colyer was on his feet now, Lundberg standing up as well, not wanting this to get out of control, he put a hand on Colyer's arm, but Colyer said, "Fuck you, narc trash. I know about you. You never did this. You never made it to detective. So where do you get the ass to second guess me? You were second rate then and now you're selling fucking furniture. Stick with the things you know."

Maitland remained seated. He said, "I know that you don't treat victims like criminals. I at least learned that." Maitland leaned forward. "Here's my problem, detective: I don't think you have any leads on this case so you're taking it out on her. Not because you think she's really guilty of anything, but because you can. It's how guys like you operate."

Maitland stayed where he was. He knew Colyer had lost his temper, but also that Colyer had hoped to incite Maitland to take a swing at him. Maitland resisted doing that and just returned an insult of his own. Now it was to Colyer and he could throw the first punch if he wanted.

If Lundberg hadn't been there, if they weren't being taped, Colyer would have done just that. But he couldn't and he knew it.

Lundberg saved him, saying, "Tempers are rising here." He looked at Maitland and added, "No thanks to you. Take her home. We'll be in touch."

Maitland and Bianca stood up and Lundberg said, "Maitland."

"What?"

"You interfere with this investigation, I'll arrest you for obstruction. You got that?"

Maitland said, "I've done nothing wrong." He regretted saying that too.

FOURTEEN

Bianca said, "What are you sorry for?"

"I don't know," Maitland said. "I think I made things worse for you."

They were in his BMW, heading back north. Maitland had said he would drive her home. Bianca had asked him if he had any cigarettes in his car. He did, gesturing to the glove box. Bianca got one out and lighted it. She cracked the window to let the smoke pull out.

Bianca shook her head. "You didn't make things worse. They were assholes. Fuck, I hate policemen."

Maitland said, "They're not all like that."

"*American* police."

Maitland said it again. "They're not all like that."

He had had this discussion with her before, under less stressful circumstances. Like many expats, Bianca had a somewhat idealistic view of her native country's police force. They're nicer, more sophisticated, more nuanced back in the old country. And somehow free of mafia corruption. A delusion.

Bianca said, "You're a funny man."

"What do you mean?"

"The Chicago police, they run you off, they were willing to frame you, and you stand up for them."

"I didn't do that. I'm just saying they're not all like that. Besides, it's not as simple as you make it out to be."

"Sometimes, things are complicated, yes," she said. "But sometimes, they are black and white. This is a black and white thing, and you are not seeing it."

Maitland said, "Are we still talking about me?"

"Yes. You."

"This is not the issue. You were almost killed."

"We get to that later. What I'm saying is that these men treat me like I've done something wrong, they treat you like you were a piece of dirt, and you defend them. Not them, but the institution. And you always do it. You always end up defending them as a whole."

Maitland thought, fucking Italian. She'd rather argue than talk about how she was pursued by men with guns. Maitland said, "Them, you mean law enforcement?"

"Yes."

"I don't do that."

"You *do* do that. *Still.* I don't understand it."

"Christ, Bianca, it's not a single, unified body. It's a job with different people doing it. There are officers like Colyer and officers like Julie. There are good and bad cops just like there are good and bad doctors."

"You were there tonight, you saw how they treated you. And yet there are times I think you have more in common with them than you do me."

"I doubt that."

"Good, bad, they're all the same."

"No, they're not."

"They're all drawn to authority and power. That's why they become policemen in the first place. They don't want to solve nothing, they just want to push people around."

"A few are like that," Maitland said. "But only a few. Most of them want to help people."

The Navy Pier came into view, the ferris wheel lit up at night. The sky above was dark and cloudy. It would be cool out there, the temperature on the lake sometimes as much as fifteen degrees lower than inland.

Maitland said, "Are you scared?"

"Yes," Bianca said. "Very."

"You've never really experienced anything like that, have you?"

"No. I don't want to, ever again." She was looking away from him, out her window at the lake. She said, "You think it would be like a movie. That someone gets shot in front of you and you would start screaming. But I couldn't. I couldn't say anything. I couldn't do anything. That man was standing there with this long gun and he looked at me. He was surprised I was there. And . . . I don't know. It was like I was nothing. A bird. And I didn't do anything. I didn't try to stop him. I didn't try to run. I just stood there . . . hoping, I guess, that he would be merciful. I'm kind of ashamed, if you want to know the truth."

"Ashamed? Why?"

"I just told you why."

It was a not uncommon reaction. Maitland said, "Did you feel you made a mistake? That you should have known better?"

"Yes. That's it."

"That you should have known better than to go to his home?"

"Yes."

"Why do you feel that?"

"Well, I thought he might misinterpret it."

"You mean that he might think you were interested in an affair?"

"Yes."

"And what signals did you give him that gave him such an idea?"

"None. But with some men, it don't make any difference."

"Well, okay. But that wouldn't be the first time you've had to deal with that, is it?"

"No."

"Was it an issue this time?"

"Yes. At the beginning. I told him I was married and not interested, but that we could continue doing business if he wanted. And he was okay with that."

"Really?"

"Yes, really. He didn't stamp his feet or get ugly like some men would. He accepted it."

"Tell me," Maitland said, "before you went to Raymond Liu's house, did you have any idea that he might be mixed up in anything illegal?"

"No."

"Did you have any idea that he might be mixed up with violent or crooked men?"

"No."

"You feel you should have known that?"

"I don't know."

"Well, you didn't. And there was no reason for you to think that you should've."

Bianca shook her head. "Excuse me?"

"What I'm saying is, these things are usually random."

"You mean it wasn't planned?"

"Oh, it was probably planned. But not by you. Do you understand?"

"No, I don't understand."

"My point is, *you* didn't do anything wrong. You did nothing to be ashamed of, nothing to feel stupid about. Cops are . . . fucked up. Not in the sense you think, but in a different sense. Some of them think things can be avoided if you're just smart enough. Maybe they were suggesting to you that you should have known better than to go to Raymond's in the first place. But that line of thought doesn't make any sense. You weren't going there to have an affair with him."

"I wasn't."

"I know. I just said that," Maitland said. "You were going there to do business with him. So there's nothing to feel ashamed about. Nothing to second guess yourself over."

"Okay."

"You're alive, aren't you?"

"Yes."

"And that's good, isn't it?"

"Yes."

Maitland looked over at her. He said, "I think so, too."

Bianca took his hand and held it. She looked at him briefly and then turned away. She said, "You are a good man, Evan."

Maitland looked at her hair and neck and the way her hip curved against the car seat. He said, "Not so much."

Bianca said, "They want me to go back tomorrow and look at photo albums. See if I recognize anyone."

"Well," Maitland said, "those would be of people who have records. Chinese people." He looked at her. "You saw three different men?"

"Yes. Two in the apartment, a third one in the alley."

"And you're sure the one in the alley was different?"

"Yes."

"And the one that got shot, he let you go?"

"Yes."

"And like you told the police, you didn't know him."

"No. Never saw him before."

"But he let you go."

"Yes."

"Did he say why?"

"No. He just said 'go.' "

"Go."

"Yes."

"But why?"

"Why? I don't know. I think they were there to kill Mr. Liu. He seemed surprised to see me. I think he might have done it if that other man hadn't come in."

"The man from the kitchen."

"Yes. They seemed to know each other. They looked at each other and the guy in the kitchen shot the first man. Then the first man shot him back. It was after that that he let me go."

"He was surprised that the other man shot him?"

"Well . . . I mean a person would always be surprised by that, wouldn't he?"

"Not always," Maitland said.

"So, you think they were working together, and there was some sort of betrayal?"

"Maybe. I mean, if he knew the man."

"I think he knew him. But, Jesus, it was all so fast."

"Bianca?"

"Yes."

"What do you know about Raymond Liu?"

"Not much. He's run that business for a long time."

"You met him at that party Saturday?"

"Yes."

"And that was the first time?"

"Yes."

Maitland said, "You called Max, didn't you?"

"Of course I called him. He's my husband."

Maitland thought, where is he now? He said, "Okay."

Bianca said, "I told him not to worry. That I was okay and that you would drive me home."

"And he's okay with that?"

"Of course he is," she said. "He knows you."

"Tomorrow," Maitland said, "Do you want me to go with you? When you see the detectives again?"

"No. I can handle them. Tomorrow, I can. Tonight was a little rough."

"Well, you can call me if you need me."

Bianca nodded in the darkness. After a moment, she said, "Did that bother you? What that policeman said to you?"

"About me being second rate, not having ever been a detective, and so forth?"

"Yes."

"Ah, a little. Homicide detectives, they're sort of the elite at metropolitan police departments. He just wanted to remind me that I wasn't one of them."

"Why would you want to be?"

Maitland said, "It's hard to explain."

She shook her head, saying something.

Maitland said, "What?"

"Silly," she said.

"What?"

"You. You're silly. That man probably hates his job. Maybe he even envies you for having got out of something he's in. And yet he came up with something shitty to say to you and you're letting it get to you. You're a grown man. You want to spend your life thinking about what might have been at a police department?"

"No."

"Then don't. And don't let yourself be bothered by little men."

Maitland looked at her for a moment. He said, "Are you trying to boss me?"

"Trying to *help* you," she said. She smiled at him then. "But sometimes, Evan, I wonder if you're worth the trouble."

FIFTEEN

Frank Chang could only drive for about a mile before he pulled over to take his jacket and shirt off and remove the Kevlar vest from beneath. It had protected him from the bullet, but there was still a yellowish-purple bruise from the impact. He breathed easier once it was off. He threw the vest in the backseat and buttoned his shirt back up and put his jacket back on. Put the car back in gear and kept going further into the south side of Chicago.

He stopped in an abandoned lot near the elevated train tracks and shut the car off. He leaned back and closed his eyes. He heard a train approach, the roar peaking as it went by, then dissipating, then gone.

He had not expected it to be Yu-shi.

He had not spoken to Yu-shi in any sort of personal way. Had not told him that he had come from Hong Kong himself when he was a little boy.

In the sixties they allowed 70,000 Chinese to come to America because of a famine in China. Frank had been little more than a toddler then, with two older brothers and one sister. From China by way of Hong Kong to an unfurnished single-room tenement in New York. No furniture, no heat. All of them lived in that room. Frank learned early to sleep perfectly still because to stir was to bump into someone else. They were called FOBs, meaning fresh off the boat.

His parents had trouble finding work. They could not apply for minimum-wage jobs at places like McDonald's because they couldn't speak English. Their options were limited to sewing shops and laundries and other dead-end work sickening to the spirit. Pay was not tracked by any government and working conditions were not monitored. Frank's father fell into gambling and committed suicide when Frank was six. The next year, Frank's sister became a prostitute. One of Frank's brothers went back to Hong Kong and the other died from lung cancer. Frank was a teenager when he was recruited by the White Lotus Triad.

He was tough and resourceful and he was a natural leader. He was respected as his father never had been. He had learned

English not from his parents but from other children. He retained his Chinese-Cantonese, but mostly to the degree he had learned it as a child. He had left Hong Kong as a child and, had he returned, he would not have been adept in the language. In a way, this set him adrift. Having lived almost all of his life in Chinatown, New York, he was not a fully assimilated American. Having limited Cantonese, he would never fully be a Hong Kong or mainland Chinese.

To the degree he could, he was contemplating this now as he thought of Yu-shi.

He had expected Hsu-shen to make a move against him. Hsu-shen had killing in his eyes and Frank had taken his bag into the bathroom and put the vest on underneath his clothes. Hsu-shen had not caught him doing this. He had been worried about Hsu-shen, but he had not thought about Yu-shi. Yu-shi of Hong Kong. Yu-shi who he had not known last week. But it was Yu-shi who had tried to kill him.

At some point, Wong or Hsu-shen had gotten to Yu-shi and persuaded him to kill him. There would have been at least two or three opportunities to have such a discussion, to make a deal. Frank was not with Yu-shi all the time. Maybe they had discussed it before he even got to Chicago.

Frank smiled to himself.

Would it have made any difference to Yu-shi if he had known that Frank had once lived in Hong Kong? Doubtful. After all, Yu-shi had been flown in to Chicago to kill two other Chinese. As had Frank Chang. Neither he nor Yu-shi had asked Wong if the men they were killing had ever lived in Hong Kong or the mainland. It wouldn't have made any difference. Foolish to think otherwise.

There was no point in being angry at Yu-shi. Yu-shi had no more betrayed him than he had Robert Wo or Raymond Liu. He had come to Chicago to do a job. At some point, that job had expanded to include the murder of Frank Chang.

But why? Was it because he had offended Wong? Was it because they didn't want to pay him? Or did it go deeper than that? Had they made an agreement with the White Lotus to have him eliminated? Was it because he had let a *gwai lo* police officer get killed? Or was it perhaps a token of respect to the Red Lantern? Yes, we killed two of yours, but we also killed the men who did it. Killed the ghosts. Just business, you see.

But it was hard to think of it just being business when he remembered the look on Hsu-shen's face. An anticipation, a blood lust. Maybe it was personal.

Yu-shi dead. Sik-ho dead. But Frank Chang was still alive. And they would know it. He could leave the city and go back to New York. But that was not an option if his own triad, the White Lotus, was involved. If that were the case, they would kill him to keep peace with Wong and his Wu-Chai. Or they might just kill him to save face. There would be no hiding in New York. Frank knew that as well as anyone. One of his duties was debt collection and more than once he had given the standard warning to those late with payment. *You have friends and your friends have friends. You have family and we know where they are too. There is no place to hide.* The speech usually worked. It was working on him now. He had gotten himself in this situation. Partly out of greed, partly out of respect to his own triad.

What was at stake here was control of the heroin trade in Chicago. Wong himself had told him that the assassins had been brought in to send a message to the Red Lantern. Using assassins from out of town because they *didn't* want a war. After the message had been delivered, Wong would perhaps sit down with the leaders of the Red Lantern and negotiate a takeover of the heroin trade. Having lost their top chemist, the Red

Lantern would be in a weak position to make much demands. From Wong's perspective, it was a measured demonstration of force.

But the assassins themselves were expendable.

Movement to his right. Shadows approaching in the dark. Now they were standing next to the Lexus, rapping on the window.

Frank hit the electric switch and rolled down the window.

It was just a couple of black guys. Around twenty or twenty-one, but no older. They were keyed up and Frank believed that at least one of them was armed, his hand in the pocket of his hooded pullover.

"What?" Frank said. His voice was sharp and commanding, no fear in it, and he hoped that would give them some hint.

It didn't. The one with the hand in his pocket said, "You got any money, boy?"

Frank took the .45 out of his pocket and set the barrel on top of the car door. He said, "Beat it."

He kept the gun there as they backed away, one of them mumbling curses, face being important to him too. But neither one of them was stupid enough or stoned enough as to be unaware that the Chinaman would pull the trigger if their own weapons were drawn. They backed up and they turned and they walked away.

When they were gone, Frank started the car and drove away.

Sixteen

Preston Wong left much of the planning of the Tasset fundraiser to his wife. Her name was Janice. She was twelve years younger than him. She was an American-born Chinese, but, like her husband, she was of Taiwanese parentage. Preston Wong had sought her out a few years ago when he had decided that he needed a wife.

She was then a corporate lawyer working for one of the larger firms in San Francisco. He appealed to her from the start. He was charming and attentive and self-assured. He was also quite rich. Janice didn't ask where the money came from. Nor did her parents. Wong told her, loosely, of his plans to start a business in Chicago. She told him that his ideas were well founded and that he would do well. They were married three months after they met. They had the traditional Chinese wedding banquet. Her parents were very happy.

Also present at the wedding was the *shan chu* of the San Francisco Wu Chai Triad. His name was Wu Tso-lin. His "American" name was Johnny Wu. It was Wu who brought Preston Wong out of Taiwan and into San Francisco. Wu gave him a Red Pole position in the San Francisco Wu-Chai and soon promoted him to deputy *shan chu.* Within a few years, Wong proposed to Wu that the Wu-Chai take over the Chicago heroin trade. Wong said that it could be done without much difficulty and in as little as five years. Once they had control of that market, annual profits could easily exceed fifty million dollars. The Wu-Chai in San Francisco and Taiwan would reap a share of the benefits. Wu agreed.

These plans were not discussed in the presence of Janice Wong. Preston Wong had never said anything relating to heroin or drugs or assassins or Wu Chai in her presence. He was aware of her intelligence. But he was also aware of her drive and her ambition. Preston had selected Janice, in part, because he knew she was attracted to power and position. He knew that she would want to share in the benefits of his life, while not inquiring as to how and where he got those benefits. He understood her vanity and, not unlike many men, was attracted to it. He also understood that on most levels she wanted the same things he did.

Money and power to be sure. But that was not the only thing. Like him, she wanted respectability. Place. Not the status of a latter-day bootlegger or greasy Latin American drug wholesaler. Something far better than that. In this goal, Janice would complement him. She would help him.

Preston Wong could admit to himself that there were some things she could do better than he. One of them was to set up a fundraiser for Congressman Tasset. She knew when to consult him and when not to. This pleased Wong. He had intentionally avoided marriage to a meek Chinese girl, her feet and temperament bound by tradition. He knew that such a wife would not serve him well in his own ambitions. Like the savvy politician, Preston Wong understood not only himself, but also the times in which he lived.

Theirs was a mutually beneficial partnership. Even so, it was not without affection. She had given him two children and they were now enrolled in one of Chicago's most prestigious private schools. When he was with his family, Preston Wong felt a pride and a contentment that he believed he had earned.

In a different way, he would feel a pride of ownership over men. Men in public office. Men like Congressman Tasset. Such ownership would give him prestige as well as protection.

Janice had prepared some notes on the status of the Tasset fundraiser and she was going over some things with her husband when his cell phone rang. Preston excused himself to take the call.

It was Hsu-shen.

They met at a back room in a restaurant that Wong owned. Hsu-shen told him what had happened, leaving in the good and the bad.

Preston Wong said, "Do you know who the woman is?"

"No. We didn't know he had a woman."

Wong said, "Shouldn't you have? He wasn't at his home. He was at his private apartment. That's where men usually do those things."

"Perhaps we should have known," Hsu-shen said. "Chang hadn't thought of it."

"You blame him?" Wong's voice was sharp and accusing, the old policeman in him coming to the fore.

Hsu-shen shrugged.

Wong said, "And she escaped?"

"Yes."

Wong sighed. He said, "What about Chang?"

"I don't know what happened. I went back to the apartment after I — after the woman escaped. There was a police car there."

"And Yu-shi?"

"I haven't heard from him."

"Is it possible that Chang killed him then?"

After a moment, Hsu-shen said, "It's possible."

Wong said, "It's not just possible. It's likely. If Yu-shi had succeeded, we would have heard from him."

"Maybe they're both dead."

"But we don't know. Someone called the police. Maybe it was the woman. Maybe it was the neighbors." Wong gave Hsu-shen a look. "I think it was the woman."

Hsu-shen said, "I'm sorry."

"That doesn't help," Wong said. "Did she see you as well?"

"No. It was too dark."

"Are you sure?" Wong said. The ex-cop talking again.

"Yes. I'm sure."

Wong didn't believe that. It had been dark and maybe all Chinese looked alike to her. But maybe they didn't. Wong said, "Was she

158

Chinese?"

"No. She was white."

And Wong felt even worse. Were the woman Chinese, she would be more likely to keep her mouth shut. More likely to refuse to call the police. But she wasn't Chinese. And there had been a police car at Liu's apartment when Hsu-shen got back.

Wong said, "Find out who she is and kill her. And get me confirmation that Frank Chang is dead."

SEVENTEEN

Maitland went to the shop early the next morning. Bianca was not there. He read the *Sun-Times,* but didn't find any mention of the murders committed in Hyde Park. He reviewed the mail and Internet messages and at nine-thirty Bianca called him and said she had to meet with the detectives to look at photographs of Asian people.

"They're expanding it apparently," she said. "To Vietnamese gangs."

Maitland said, "They said that?"

"They said anything's possible. They think it was probably a home invading."

"Home invasion," Maitland said. "That's just a term for robbing a house. Did it seem like that to you?"

"Well, I don't know if they took anything. I do remember that they just shot the man right away. They didn't ask him where he kept his gold or anything. Evan, do these guys know what they're doing?"

"I don't know. Were they rude this time?"

"No. I think they're afraid I'm going to bring a lawyer with me."

"You can, you know."

"I'll think about it. But . . . for now, I'll cooperate."

"I can come."

"No. Just stay there and take care of things, okay?"

"Okay. How's Max with this?"

"He was pretty shaken up. He said he was sorry for not coming to the police station."

"But you told him not to."

"I know. But he's still sorry. I had to — you know, hide some things from him."

"Like what?"

"Well, the way the police acted. I don't want him upset too."

"Is he worried about your safety?"

"Yes."

Maitland said, "Do you guys have a gun in the house?" He was pretty sure he knew the answer.

"No," she said. The Euro-liberal offense in her tone just at the thought of it. Like asking a bible-thumper if they kept pornography under the bed.

"You should probably get one," Maitland said. "You can tell Max I said that."

Bianca said, "I will, but he's . . . he's not

going to do that."

"Not even for you?"

"Evan, don't say things like that. I don't think this involves me anyway. I was just at the wrong place at the wrong time."

"It wouldn't be like having an evil spirit in the home, Bianca. A weapon is just a tool."

"Evan, I think the world of you. But you don't see things the way we see them."

"I think I see them as they are. Try to, anyway."

"But your perception, it's dark and violent. We can't live like that."

"It's not as dramatic as all that," Maitland said. He paused. Sometimes he liked to goad her, sometimes he didn't. Now he said, "Listen, I'm not trying to frighten you or anything. The odds of you needing it are probably minimal. I'm just being cautious, that's all."

"If they're minimal, there's no point. Listen, I have to go. I'll call you later, huh?"

"Okay. Good luck."

He hung up the phone, a little irritated. He had had similar discussions with her in the past. She could be stubborn on certain subjects, one of them being guns. Most of her adult life spent in America, but her sensibility still very Italian, still very European. She liked argument and he was resistant to it. Still, she could be persistent and drag him into these discussions. More than once he had been told that America was a violent country, obsessed with guns and westerns and John Wayne and when a European brings up John Wayne, you know you've got trouble. America wasn't the land of Jefferson and Washington and Jackson Pollock and Bill Haley and the Comets, it was the land of John Wayne and Rambo. That is, two movie stars neither one of whom had seen military service.

Generally, this didn't bother Maitland. His was not a political nature. But he was put off by people who valued ideology over sound judgment and, moreover, reality. Bianca's husband was no European. What he was was a typical metropolitan liberal. And his distaste for guns was more visceral and cultural than it was intellectual. Second Amendment, violent crime, self-defense, and armed Swiss neutrality, whatever . . . guns were for losers and psychos and rednecks and people of little education and of course any intelligent person would know that.

Still, Maitland had no beef with Max. He liked him, actually. Though he sensed in Max a discomfort with him. Perhaps this was because Max had figured out Maitland was attracted to his wife. Or perhaps the discomfort stemmed from Maitland being something of an enigma himself. Max may have wondered, how was it that his wife could be friends with an ex-policeman, a man who still chased people with guns? While Maitland wondered what had drawn Bianca to Max in the first place and why she remained with him. Each man was tied to the same woman and each man probably had difficulty understanding the other. Bianca was a woman of reserve and she did not discuss the status of her marriage with Maitland. Nor did Maitland ask.

But you don't see things the way we see them.

That was what she had told him. Not "I," but "we." Her and her husband on one side, him on the other. It was the way it was, Maitland thought. And probably the way it should be.

Maitland dialed a number.

She answered on the third ring.

"Evan?"

"Hi. Listen, Bianca was a witness to a shooting last night. In Hyde Park. Do you know anything about it?"

Julie said, "No. What happened?"

"She went to a man's apartment to look at some antique photos. It was work. And some men burst into the apartment and killed him. She got away, though."

"Jesus. Is she okay?"

"Yes. Detectives Colyer and Lundberg questioned her afterward. Can you look into it for me?"

"Sure. Let me make some calls. Can you meet me for lunch?"

"I'm sorry, I can't. Bianca's downtown looking at arrest photos. I have to mind the store. Can I call you this afternoon?"

"That's fine. I'll talk to you then."

Po-han was twenty-two years old, but could pass for eighteen, young and of slight build. He had worn a red scarf when he had been a triad recruit, but was told to put it away today.

He was sitting in the backseat of a Lincoln Continental, riding downtown. Hsu-shen was in the front, Big Kon behind the wheel.

Hsu-shen said, "You've seen the photos?"

Po-han said, "Yes." The photographs of the killers from Hong Kong and New York, respectively. One of them was dead and the other one was alive, but they weren't sure which was which.

Hsu-shen said, "They're going to ask you who you are, you give them a name. Not your own. Tell them something common. Chin or Lin. They'll write it down, maybe, but it won't matter. They're going to think you're a member of a gang, a punk. That's okay. Let them think it. You don't have any identification on you, do you?"

"No."

"Good. Check again to be sure."

Po-han checked his pockets as Hsu-shen went on.

"After you see the body, tell them it's not who you were looking for. It's not your friend. Act relieved. And then get out of there."

The city morgue was within sight now.

Hsu-shen said to his driver, "Pull over here." He turned around to Po-han. "No identification?"

"No," Po-han said.

"Good. Get out here. We expect to hear from you within an hour. If you get detained, don't call me. Under no circumstances give out your name. Understand?"

"Yes, Hsu-shen."

It went more or less as planned. Po-han told the people at the front desk that he hadn't seen his friend Victor for a few days and he was worried that he might be dead. Victor who? And Po-han made his face a puzzle and acted like he had great difficulty with the English language. Victor, he repeated and finally said, "Lu." Like it would help. "He Chinese," Po-han said. "No driver license." His own English was considerably more broken and stilted than it had been in the car.

They took him downstairs and led him to a drawer and pulled out a slab with a corpse on it. Po-han studied it for a minute. He saw the Hong Kong dragon on the corpse's wrist. Then he shook his head.

"No," he said. "Na him, na him."

"Sorry," the clerk said. He closed the drawer and escorted Po-han to the exit.

It was easier than he thought it would be.

He walked for four blocks before he called Hsu-shen on his cell phone. Gave him a location and they picked him up fifteen minutes later.

Po-han got in the car and said, "It's Yu-shi."

At eleven o'clock, the two Bobs came in, Bob Jensen and Bob Sfranski, a gay couple who had been regular customers for years. They had an appointment with Bianca, but were okay with Evan as they knew him as well. Evan showed them the 19th-century butcher's table with the original Carerra marble, cast iron gallery, and brass balls. Bob Sfranski made some joke at that last part and Bob Jensen rolled his eyes and told him to hush up, he was always embarrassing him, and Bob Sfranski said Bob Jensen needed to stop being so grumpy. They asked where Bianca was and Maitland told them there was a minor emergency and that she had to go downtown, but that she wasn't hurt and everything would be fine. Bob Jensen said he loved the butcher's table and that it would look great in their sunroom with a couple of ceramic cups on top and he thought their price was fair but that he wanted to think about it for a couple of days. Maitland said that was fine and that they would hold it till Friday if they wanted, but couldn't promise to do so much longer. Bob Jensen said Maitland was a gentleman and that he appreciated that very much.

Maitland said, "How is Arthur doing?"

Arthur was Bob Jensen's mixed collie-labrador. He was sixteen years old and Bob Jensen had been with him all that time. Longer than he'd been with Bob Sfranski.

Bob Jensen said, "Oh, he's getting around, but barely. The poor thing's arthritis is wearing him down. But . . . when you put the food on the kitchen floor, he comes over and eats it, his tail wagging. And he's better with the medication. So, as long as he's doing that, I'm not going to put him down. I'm just not."

"I understand that," Maitland said.

Bob Jensen said, "Do you have a dog?"

"No," Maitland said. "I did when I was a kid. And we put her down when she couldn't see anymore. She was fifteen. You're doing the right thing."

"I know." His voice caught at the end. "It's hard to see him suffer that way, though."

"I know," Maitland said. "But you've had a lot of good years with him and he recognizes that too."

The two Bobs exchanged a look and then Bob Jensen drifted off. He was the older of the couple, somewhat aristocratic with the look of the theater about him. Bob Sfranski was younger and flamboyant. Two men that Maitland would have had little contact with before getting into the antique business, but one adapted.

Bob Sfranski said, "Evan, he wants the table. He just always has to do this . . . waiting period thing. You know how he is."

"Don't worry about it," Maitland said. "No pressure."

Bob Sfranski was looking at him now, a troubled expression on his face. He said, "Bianca is okay, isn't she?"

"She's fine," Maitland said.

Maitland locked the shop at twelve-thirty and walked down the street to a deli to buy a sandwich and chips. He brought it back to the shop and ate it at his desk. He was thinking about Bob Sfranski asking if Bianca was okay, wondering if his own anxiety was showing. Would Bob Sfranski be able to persuade Bianca of the benefits of gun ownership?

He lifted his head up when he heard the door open and saw Bianca come in. He was conscious of his heart beating. It was the same relief a father feels when his child has finally come home late at night, safe. Or that a husband feels for his wife. Maitland felt embarrassed.

She came into the office.

Maitland said, "How did it go?"

"Shitty. Man, those guys don't know anything."

"They show you pictures?"

"Yes. But I didn't recognize any of them. They kept saying, 'Are you sure? Are you sure?' Like I'm retarded or something."

"Well . . ."

"And they raise their voices when they talk to me. Not like they shouting, but like I'm hard of hearing. I guess because of my accent, they think I don't understand English."

"I don't know about that . . ."

"Don't say that to me. You weren't there. For God's sake, I been in this country twenty years and they act like I'm here on a green card."

"You're right. I wasn't there."

She put her bag on her own desk and sat down. She looked at him and said, "Sorry."

"It's okay." Maitland said, "Do they have any leads?"

"God, I don't know. When I'm there, it's like I'm a bother to them. They still think I had something going on with him."

"With Raymond Liu?"

"Yes. I mean, they don't say it directly. But it's like they thought I was keeping something from them."

"I'm sorry, Bianca."

"It's not your fault. Most of those photos they showed me, they look like kids."

"Gang members?"

"I think so," she said. "Tattoos, headbands . . . they didn't look nothing like the men I saw. Not even close."

"But Asian."

"Yes, Asian," she said. "They showed me a picture of this one guy, though, who was older. Much older. Asked if I'd ever seen him before. I looked at it and said no, I hadn't, and they said, 'You sure?' Like I was hiding it from them."

"Was it a booking photo?"

"A what?"

"A photo they take when they arrest someone. You know, from the front and the side."

"No. It looked like it was taken outside. He was getting into a car."

Maitland said, "An older man?"

"Yes."

Maitland flipped through the newspaper and found the article on the Ravinia's shooting. A photo of the dead DEA agent, but not one of the other victims. He found the name of the older man.

Maitland said, "Was this older man named Robert Wo?"

"Yes. Why?"

Maitland pushed the newspaper over to her. He said, "He was one of the men killed at Ravinia's Sunday night."

"Oh," she said.

"Did they tell you that?"

"No."

"They didn't? They didn't tell you that?"

"I don't know," she said. "Maybe they didn't think it was important."

■ ■ ■ ■

"And of course it's important," Maitland said.

Julie Ciskowski said, "Maybe they're not sure it's linked."

"If they thought that, why would they show it to her?"

They were in Maitland's apartment now. Julie had called him back at the store about a half hour after Bianca got back. She said she'd made some calls and had some information and maybe they could discuss it at his place after he finished work. Maitland said that was okay, thinking it would put her in his apartment for the first time in a couple of days. Though that was the least of the troubles these days.

Maitland cooked dinner. Chicken seasoned with garlic and lemon pepper, boiled potatoes, salad and bread. Julie sipped a glass of wine while he prepared it and they continued the thread of conversation through the meal.

Julie said, "Look, one Asian man gets killed at Ravinia's and the next night another Asian gets killed in Hyde Park. It's not like they all know each other."

"Okay," Maitland said, "maybe they didn't

know each other. But the detectives must have thought there was some connection if they showed that photo to Bianca."

"Maybe," Julie said. "Maybe, Evan. But maybe it's just a theory."

"You taking their side?"

Julie sighed. "Evan, what are you saying something like that for? There is no side. You talk as if the detectives are the ones who're endangering Bianca. They're just doing their job."

"Did you know they asked her if she was having an affair with Raymond Liu?"

"So what? I'd've probably asked her the same thing." She caught his look and said, "Evan, you would have too if you were in their place. It's a criminal investigation, not a tea party."

"Well, she wasn't."

"Okay, she wasn't."

"Christ," Maitland said. His face was in his hands. "Is it a gang thing?"

"Well, they don't know for sure," Julie said. "Not exactly a gang."

Maitland looked up, not liking the sound of that one bit. He said, "What do you mean?"

"Are you familiar with something called a triad?"

"A triad. That's Chinese, right?"

"Yes."

After a moment, Maitland said, "Like a Chinese mafia."

"Yes."

"Oh, God. Is that was this is?"

"Maybe. Evan, they don't know for sure. The victims were clean. Neither one had an arrest record. But DEA had been tracking Wo for some time. They believed he was a chemist for an organization called the Red Lantern Triad. When I say chemist, I mean heroin chemist. He was the one that —"

"I know what they do."

"He was, allegedly, the Red Lantern's top chemist. He'll be very difficult to replace. As for Liu, they're not sure about him."

"Not sure what he did?"

"DEA is being territorial, as usual. They want to retain control of the Wo investigation. That's understandable, as they lost a man who was tailing him. They don't seem that interested in Liu."

"Was Liu involved in heroin trafficking?"

"No record that he was. At least, no record Chicago PD is aware of."

"Was he a member of the Red Lantern?"

"They're not sure. But he ran a Chinese art and antique boutique. And it's not unusual to use such a business to launder money. Drug profits."

"Oh, no," Maitland said. Drug traffickers, Chinese mafia, guns, and vendettas. Bianca in the middle of it. Maitland remembered the conversation they'd had just, Christ, a couple of days ago. Her saying she was going to be meeting with Raymond Liu, Maitland telling her good luck with all that.

Maitland said, "I should have known. I should have said something."

"What do you mean?" Julie said.

"She told me she was meeting with him. I should have warned her."

"Warned her of what? You didn't know anything. Evan, Chicago PD doesn't even have a file on the guy. He's clean."

"But I should have known."

"How could you know? Evan, why are you doing this to yourself? A bad thing happened to your business partner, and you're going to take responsibility for it?"

"She was meeting with a fucking *criminal,* Julie. If I'd gone to that party with her, met the guy when she did, I could've done something."

"Done what? Would the hairs on your neck have tingled and let you know he was trouble?"

"Maybe."

"Maybe not. Probably not. Evan, he was a respectable civilian. If you think you'd've

176

automatically seen through that, you give yourself too much credit. Sorry, but you do."

Maitland shrugged. Julie thought it would have been no big thing for him to have agreed with her then, but he wouldn't do it. He could be stubborn sometimes.

But looking at him now, she wondered if she had ever seen him so worried.

When she first met him, he was recovering from a gunshot wound that took out one of his lungs. He was still using a cane to get around and his breath was short enough that he had to rest halfway through the climb on his own fire escape. Jamaicans wanting to kill him and asshole cops wanting to pin an accessory to murder charge on him.

Yet he hadn't seemed rattled then. It was as if his previous life experiences had been harsh enough that he thought, *what else can you do to me you haven't already done?* A courage, yes, but a sort of obstinate arrogance too. His mindset being that a Jamaican posse and Terry Specht simply weren't good enough to bring him down. This from a man who, at that time, couldn't even climb a set of stairs without taking a break in between.

But it wasn't about him now. It was about someone else.

Julie said, "Evan?"

"Yes."

"Can I ask you something?"

"What?"

"You went to the police station with Bianca that night?"

"Yeah."

"So she called you?"

"Yeah."

"Did she call you before she called her husband?"

"What?" Maitland said. He was getting the drift of this, but only just.

"Did she call you before she called her husband?"

"I don't know. What difference does it make?"

Julie said, "It makes a difference to me."

There was a silence between them then, Julie being a detective, but not so much a police officer now and Maitland respected her too much to avoid her eyes. He met her expression and remained quiet for a few moments.

Then he said, "There's nothing improper . . . there's nothing going on there."

Julie said, "I'm not saying it would be improper."

"I know what you're saying. She's a good friend and someone I care very much about.

That's all."

"You've known her longer than you've known me."

"I know that. But that's not . . . that's not the same."

Julie said, "No, it's not."

And she meant something by that too. But Maitland couldn't be sure, and he made a quick decision not to push it.

Julie said, "I won't ask you any more about it, okay?"

"Okay."

As if to confirm her promise, Julie stood up and cleared the dishes. Moments later, Maitland heard the water running in the kitchen sink. He left her in the kitchen and walked out to the living room and turned on the television. They were separated for some time and then she walked out of the kitchen and said, "Do you want to go to bed?"

He had to regard her for a moment to see if she meant with or without her. She meant with her.

"Okay," Maitland said.

This time, it was her that initiated the lovemaking. They did not say much to each other after it was done and soon they were both asleep.

EIGHTEEN

They grabbed Stanley Tung in the parking lot of a *fan tan* casino. He was getting his car keys out of his pocket when the Lincoln Continental screeched up to a halt and Big Kon and two other men swarmed him and he gave little resistance as they shoved him into the backseat and took off.

They did not blindfold him or say anything to him. Nor did Stanley Tung ask them questions. It had been less than twenty-four hours since Mister Liu had been killed. Mister Liu was his boss. Stanley Tung tried to avoid weeping, thinking that maybe this was his time too, but thinking something worse too. He was familiar with the triads.

They drove south to a set of morbid-looking tenements. Pulled him out of the car there and prodded him up three flights of stairs. Big Kon knocked on a door three times and someone on the other side unlocked it and let them in.

It was Hsu-shen, another man with him.

"Ah, Mister Tung," Hsu-shen said. "We've been waiting for you."

Big Kon gave Stanley Tung a shove and then followed him into the apartment. There was trash on the floor, plaster falling off the walls. The smell of sweat and urine, fear and dread.

"Come here," Hsu-shen said. "We have something to show you."

Stanley Tung felt a horror drop through his gullet even before he was led to the kitchen. For he knew the triad ways. Big Kon shoved him again, amidst the laughter and knowing smiles of the men around him.

And there she was. His fifteen-year-old daughter, lying on the kitchen floor. Her arms were tied behind her back. Another rope had been noosed around her neck and was tied loosely to a weight bench. The rope was slack, but it had only to be pulled over the bar to strangle her to death. She was facedown.

Stanley Tung began to sob.

Hsu-shen said, "We haven't yet, Tung. We don't rape the girl until her father is here to see it. You know how it works."

Tung groaning now. Helpless, horrified.

Hsu-shen said, "We haven't even severed

her finger. See? See how civilized we have been? We have been generous to you. And your family. Do you agree?"

After a moment, Tung nodded.

Hsu-shen said, "These men have waited. They are hungry. Like wolves, huh? I think we start with Big Kon, huh?"

Tung was crying now.

Hsu-shen said, "You understand the importance of family, don't you?"

". . . yes."

"A man who puts others before his family dishonors his family. Yes?"

"Yes."

"Yes. He dishonors his family. He shames them. Stands by and watches them being shamed," Hsu-shen said. "But it need not be. Do you understand?"

"Yes."

"Good. Answer the next question correctly and you can spare yourself this shame. Understand?"

"Yes."

"Tell me now, who was the woman Liu brought to his apartment?"

Tung said, "He wrote it down in his appointment book. Her name is Bianca Garibaldi."

NINETEEN

Frank Chang parked the car in a vacant lot in South Chicago and managed to sleep for a couple of hours. He awoke and checked the magazine on his .45 and saw that it had four bullets left. He had no spare. He thought then of the men who had rapped on the car window last night and what would have happened if they had come back with friends. Armed friends.

Frank drove around the area. More vacant lots, abandoned buildings, townhouses that had once been beautiful on wide boulevards with beat-up automobiles lining the sides. All about the deep brown hue of poverty.

There was poverty in Chinatown as well. But it was a different kind. There were wide open spaces here, but there was no bustle, no constant commerce to cover up the despair. It depressed even him.

He had no cellular phone with him. That was typical when he was on a job. No phone, no identification. He would use those things when he went back to traveling. He had cash though. About two thousand dollars in twenties and fifties. It could have been lifted from him last night if he hadn't been armed.

He slowed the car to a stop when he saw a pay phone outside of a Church's Fried Chicken. Looked at it for a moment while he sat in the car.

He thought, you can call Chol Soo and tell him what happened. Call him and say that Wong's men betrayed him and had tried to kill him, but he had seen it coming and now he was alive and what should he do now?

Chol Soo might say that he'd have to call him back later. And then Chol Soo would get off the telephone and call Fong and then what?

Then Frank would have to wait till they told him what to do.

But what if Fong had sanctioned the attempt on Frank's life? What if Fong had told Preston Wong that, yes, if Frank was being troublesome, by all means do what you need to do.

Would Fong have done that?

Fong, like Frank and Chol Soo, had taken the 36 oaths of loyalty to the White Lotus

Triad. One of those oaths strictly forbade betraying a brother member. If a man betrayed that oath, he was subject to death by a myriad of swords.

But somehow those rules didn't always apply to the men at the top. Fong was the boss, Frank a mere Red Pole. Frank was replaceable. Another one of the oaths was that a member was to accept his punishment and not place blame on his brothers.

Preston Wong was deputy *shan chu* of the Wu Chai, not the White Lotus. But if Fong had made agreements with the Wu Chai, that could change things. Indeed, Fong may have made his agreements with the top boss in San Francisco, leaving Wong out of it altogether. Would Fong have sacrificed Frank for money or a piece of the heroin trade? Would he have done it just to maintain peace with the Wu Chai?

Maybe Chol Soo would know the answer to these questions. But if he did, he would not be likely to speak openly about it. He might tell Frank to go and wait at a certain corner at a certain time and be shot by Hsu-shen and his men.

Or, and this could be worse, Chol Soo might ask if Frank got his fifty thousand dollars. And when Frank said that, no, he had not, Chol Soo could say that failure to gain payment had cost the White Lotus face.

Frank went through these things, turning them over and looking at them from different angles, and finally he concluded that it was better not to call Chol Soo at this time. If Chol Soo or Fong gave him an order, it would be a White Lotus order and he would have to abide by it. But if there was no communication, he could act on his own. He could justifiably claim ignorance. He could do himself and Fong a favor.

Certainly himself. And perhaps set the record straight with Preston Wong and his apes. Settle it before he left town.

Yes.

Get the fifty thousand from Wong and then go back to New York. Then pay his tribute to Fong and act like nothing out of the ordinary happened. Fong would have face under that scenario. As would Frank.

But he wouldn't be able to face the apes without ammunition. Bluffing a couple of black kids was one thing, but it wouldn't work on a man like Hsu-shen.

Frank looked back at the pay phone. There was a young man using it now. A black male wearing the required bling. He hung up the phone and walked to a Jeep Cherokee and started it.

Frank watched the Cherokee motor away

in the rearview mirror. He started the Lexus, made a U-turn, and followed.

Frank kept about a half block behind the Cherokee. Followed it for about two miles until the Cherokee slowed and made a U-turn and Frank kept going, passed him, and looked in the rearview mirror again. The Cherokee was pulling up to the curb now, the kid parking it.

Frank pulled over. Watched in his mirror as the kid got out of the Cherokee and walked up the stairs of an old white gray-stone mansion. A building that had probably been worth something before the Second World War and the suburban shift. Now it was run down, boards covering the windows on the first floor.

Frank waited. He would be patient. If this wasn't a crackhouse, there would be another one within a mile.

It took only five minutes. Then the kid was walking down the stairs and getting back into his Cherokee. He started it and drove away.

Frank got out of the Lexus. He walked to the graystone mansion. He did not slow his pace as it came in front of him, but kept going. He glanced at the front door and the crack of window on the side of the board.

Enough space to see through. He kept walking until he got about two houses away and saw a staircase going down to a basement home. He went down there and crouched.

He had to wait almost a half-hour before another customer came. Another young black man, but this one was big in the shoulders and the stomach. That was a good thing, Frank thought.

The man got to the front of the steps and Frank came out of his hiding place and began walking toward him. The guy gave Frank a hard look, but only that, and Frank kept his head down, showing the guy a scared little Chink and then the man was going up the steps and Frank quickly turned and went up after him. And then they were both at the door and Frank was right on him, the .45 sticking in the guy's back.

"Yeah," Frank said. "It's a gun."

The guy tensed up. He said, "You a cop?"

"No. Keep moving."

The guy knocked on the door. There was a voice saying, "Yeah?"

Frank poked the man in the kidneys with the gun. His voice low, he said, "Get me in there or you die. Got it?"

The guy said, "Hey Justin, it's Colby. Let me in, man."

There was the sound of the door being

unlocked and when Frank saw the crack he shoved the man through, knocking the man down, Colby going on top of him. Frank stepped in and kicked the door shut behind him. There were two other guys on the couch, looking up in surprise. A girl on a recliner chair holding a pipe, her eyes still on the large screen television.

One of the kids on the couch started yelling, "What the hell?" and another one got up to run, but Frank pointed the .45 at him and told him to sit down.

The smaller black guy on the couch was wearing an Italian T-shirt, a wife beater, and he seemed to be the one in charge. He said in a tired voice, "Man, is this a raid?"

"No," Frank said. "Just keep your seat."

"You here to rob us? 'Cause we ain't got nothing."

Justin was telling Colby to get his big fuckin' ass off him, thinking something may have been broken.

Frank said to them, "Don't get up. Just roll over on your back and stay there. Both of you. Yeah, like that."

The one in the T-shirt said, "Man, you here to rob us, ain't you?"

Frank held up the gun. He said, "You see this?"

"Yeah, I see it."

"It's a .45."

"Yeah?"

"You got rounds for a .45?"

"Ammunition? You mean to tell me that ain't loaded?"

"It's loaded."

"Yeah, you fucking lying too."

"I've got enough to kill all of you. But if I start firing, you'll be the first."

"Man, where you from? Colby, get that bitch, will you?"

The guy wearing the T-shirt was named Curtis Deon. He was brave and reckless in the way that the coked-up can be, but his man Colby was closer to this Oriental dude and he saw something in the eyes and the body language that made him hesitate. Colby was on his back and now he started to sit up and take the Oriental in his sight, sizing him up. The Oriental looking down at him now, a patient expression on his face. Colby waited for the warning, something like "don't do it," but it wasn't coming and then Curtis Deon's boy Marvin came off the couch across the table to rush the man instead and the man raised the gun and shot Marvin in the leg.

Colby stayed on the floor.

Frank shook his head. He said to Curtis Deon, "That was your fault."

Marvin was rolling on the ground, grabbing his leg and screaming. The smell of gunsmoke in the tight, dirty room, the shot still echoing. The girl coming out of her daze now. Curtis Deon wore a different expression, his hands up in submission.

Curtis Deon said, "You want money, man. Take it. Take it."

"I need guns and ammunition."

"Man, I don't have no .45. I got a couple of nine millimeters. A Lorcin and a Browning. You can have 'em."

"You got rounds for the Browning?"

"Yeah. I got a box."

"I'll take that then. Where is it?"

"In the kitchen."

Frank turned to the girl. "You. Get it," he said.

Curtis Deon said, "Go on, get it."

Frank said to her, "You come back with the gun and the rounds. You hold that gun by the barrel with your thumb and two fingers. I see you holding it any other way, I'll kill you."

"Go on," Curtis Deon said.

She came back with the box and the gun between her thumb and fingers. Frank said, "Put it in that McDonald's bag. Go on."

She did so.

Frank said, "Now hand it to me. Don't

get in front of me . . . Now sit down. No, on the floor. There." He said to Curtis Deon, "You too. On the floor. Get on your back."

Curtis Deon said, "You're going to kill us all, ain't you?"

"You don't get on the floor, I'll kill *you.*"

Curtis Deon waited a moment before he got to the floor, stretching it to save his own face. After he did, Frank took his cell phone off his belt.

Frank said, "I'm going to wait outside that door for five minutes. I see anyone coming out, I'll kill them."

He backed out of the room and onto the steps. He stepped down them, his eyes on the door. Then he walked back to his car.

TWENTY

They snuck Johnny Wu into Chicago by way of an airport in Rockford. A chartered jet and then he was in a car with two of his bodyguards. They rode for about forty minutes and then they were at a ranch house surrounded by white fences. Wu saw a girl riding a horse in the pasture. They parked the car and a woman let them into the house. She was Chinese and she asked Wu if he would like some tea.

Wu said that would be nice. The woman said they could sit outside by the swimming pool as the day was not so hot. Wu accepted the offer and minutes later he and his two men were at a table with an umbrella giving them shade.

A glass door to a bedroom slid open and Preston Wong stepped out. He walked over and took a seat at the table. Johnny Wu kept his eyes on the swimming pool. The water was blue and flat, no one in it.

Wu said, "I never learned how to swim. Did you know that?"

Preston Wong said, "No, *shan chu.* You were busy, I suppose."

"A boy comes from Hong Kong, lives most of his life in San Francisco, and he never learns to swim. My children, when they were younger, they used to complain that they didn't have a pool. They thought everyone in California should have a pool. They want space. Americans. My children are Americans. We don't seem to be able to control them. We want them to remain Chinese, but they want pools and cars and skateboards."

"They are children," Wong said. He was aware that Wu's grown children were a disappointment to him. To a degree, Wong had subtly exploited this. He was about the same age as Wu's only son, who was a hothead lacking any intelligence or good judgment. Wong was able to take over the Wu-Chai, able to run Chicago. Wu's son had been unmanageable since childhood. A punk at twelve is usually still a punk at forty.

Wu took his eyes off the pool. He said, "I have been talking with Cho-jen." The leader of the Red Lantern Triad. The boss of the two men that had been killed.

"Okay," Wong said. "Is he ready to accept

reasonable terms?"

Wu paused. He said, "He is ready to discuss them. I told him that the Wu-Chai was not seeking a war. Only what was reasonable. I know Cho-jen. He wants to accept this. He wants to have this behind him. But he doesn't want to lose face with his own people either. He's lost his top chemist and his chief money launderer. He can, in time, replace Liu. Wo . . . is not so easy to replace. Perhaps impossible to replace. He was a rare talent."

"That was why he had to be eliminated," Wong said. "Half measures don't work."

"He knows that," Wu said. "But he doesn't want to accept it too soon. So . . . he's searching for things to complain about."

"Such as?"

"An American policeman was killed. He's concerned about that."

"That was an accident. Besides, it's not his concern."

"I know it's not. But as I said, he's nitpicking. He's stressing that the Wu-Chai is . . . lax. He's not saying things aloud, of course. But what he is suggesting is that we are second rate. Unprofessional."

"Because of a dead federal agent?"

Wu made a shrugging gesture. "He needs to complain about something."

Wong said, "All of the men involved in that are gone. The police can investigate all they like, but they're not going to find anything."

"That's what I told him. I told him there are no loose ends."

"There aren't."

Wu said, "We'll let him alone for a few days. We will not respond specifically to his grievances. In time, he will realize that there is nothing he can do but cooperate with us. Then we'll go through the charade of a negotiation and he can concede defeat and keep face. I estimate we can have a meeting by next week."

Wong said, "Next week?"

"Yes. Things will have settled down by then, don't you think?"

"Of course," Wong said.

"Strangely enough," Wu said, "we are aided by our enemies, the Colombians. Cho-jen knows that the triads must stick together to retain control of the heroin market. Otherwise, the Colombians will fill the void. We offer Cho-jen protection against outside forces."

"Perhaps it is not so strange," Wong said. "History is full of such alliances. There should be no shame in it."

Wu nodded and after a moment, said,

"You've had Chicago now for five years, correct?"

"Yes, about that."

"Cold winters," Wu said. "I don't think I could ever get used to it." He gestured to his two men and they started to leave.

After Wu was gone, Wong lighted a cigarette. Sometimes, he liked to have one with his tea. He did not often smoke at home because his wife did not like it. She was in many ways more American than Chinese. Her traditional Chinese outfits were more for show than anything else. Wong was aware of this and, for the most part, was okay with it. She did not push him or attempt to control him. Though most men in his position would have kept a mistress, Wong never had. In part, because it didn't interest him. But he was also aware that the Chinese man risked losing face when he got involved with mistresses and prostitutes. The kept woman would more often than not have relations with another man and if the triad community became aware of this, it was an embarrassment, perhaps even a humiliation. Such things were too damaging to a man of his position and power. Wong's wife once told him that he was Victorian in his sensibilities, unaware of the irony in this charge.

It was when she said things like this that Wong thought she was hopelessly American. She had read the Amy Tan books and the Phoebe Eng warrior within nonsense, but her cultural worldview was that of a typical, liberal arts–educated American. That is, hopelessly ignorant of history. Calling him Victorian, for example. Unaware that Queen Victoria was not someone especially admired in China. It was under her reign that England fought China in the Opium Wars. China, underpowered and underarmed, never stood a chance. And for what purpose was this war fought? So England could continue to import opium from India into China. Turning a nation of people into hopeless addicts. Retarding their spirit and corrupting their civilization. When the Japanese invaded in the thirties, the Chinese could barely defend themselves. Now the western civilizations spoke of drug cartels like they were criminals and thugs, conveniently forgetting that the British Empire was once the biggest drug cartel of all.

Now it was those same western civilizations bemoaning the fact that you just couldn't do business with the Chinese. They were all thieves, they said, devoid of honor and decency. For the Chinese, everything was about money.

Well, Wong thought, perhaps that was true. But no more so there than anyplace else. And as for the Americans' so-called love of freedom of expression and whatever it was they called "free trade," their hypocrisy was unbounded. The Americans liked to complain about Chinese suppression, but it was American companies that had built the Internet technology that not only prevented the Chinese from accessing websites critical of Mother China, but also tracked e-mail correspondence showing any favorable tendency toward democratic reform. Only the Americans could do something like that and then claim, with a straight face, that American business would eventually "liberalize" China. Actually, it had strengthened the State's ability to oppress its citizens.

This human condition did not depress Preston Wong. He was not a romantic. He had never entertained such illusions as democracy or freedom or even justice. He did not love and, he believed, he did not hate. The world was a harsh place and one must do his best to succeed in it.

When he was a young man, he had become a policeman in Taipei, Taiwan, because it offered him the best opportunity available at that time. He was recruited by the Wu-Chai Triad during his first year. He was not the first cop to be approached and he would not be the last. But in Taiwan and mainland China, it was not particularly unusual to be both a policeman and a member of a triad. Indeed, many police officers considered the triads patriotic organizations. Using his contacts and powers as a police sergeant, Wong helped ensure safe passage of heroin shipments to Amsterdam, Vancouver, and San Francisco. When he discovered that there was an informant working for the Taipei police, he informed his local *shan chu*. The Wu Chai thanked him for his loyalty. And then, as if to ensure that loyalty, they requested that Wong kill the informant himself. Wong did so without hesitation. After that, he was made a Red Pole.

A couple of years after that, the Taipei police began to investigate him. He fled to San Francisco and began working for Johnny Wu. In San Francisco, he continued his role as Red Pole and sometime assassin. He became valuable to Wu as an administrator and natural leader.

Wong was aware that Wu probably had personal reasons for shipping him out to Chicago: Wu was afraid that Wong might take over San Francisco. Wu could either let that happen or he could kill him. Wu made the more reasonable choice. Now Chicago was becoming Wu Chai territory under the administration of Preston Wong. Wu had been diplomatic about it, saying today that Chicago was "too cold" for him anyway.

But to have power, one had to have money. And that was the point of controlling the Chicago heroin market. Wu was right. In time, Cho-jen would understand this. Perhaps years from now, someone else would wrest control from the Wu-Chai. Or attempt to.

But Preston Wong allowed himself to think he was smarter than Cho-jen. And Johnny Wu. He would make himself better protected than they had. Buying Congressman Tasset was just the start of this.

Wong had not told Wu about Congressman Tasset. Nor had he told Wu about Frank Chang being alive and unaccounted for or about the white woman who had been in Raymond Liu's apartment. It would have displeased Wu, made him uneasy. He had told Wu there were no loose ends.

Next week, Wu had said. *Things will have settled down by then, don't you think?*

"Of course," Wong said.

Of course. They would kill the woman by then.

TWENTY-ONE

Big Kon asked why they couldn't just go in there and shoot her. Hsu-shen said there could be customers in there and they would have to kill them too. Wong had said he didn't want a Golden Dragon–type public bloodbath. The disappearance of one woman could be a mystery and only that. But a mass murder would make the front page and commissions would be created to "do something" about a sudden crime wave.

They were in a Chrysler parked down the street from the woman's shop, the evening pulling down the sun. Hsu-shen sat up front with Po-han behind the wheel and this time it was Big Kon in the backseat. There was a towel on the front seat between Hsu-shen and Po-han. Underneath the towel were two handguns.

They had left the Lincoln downtown. Po-han had stolen the Chrysler about four hours earlier. Wong had said it would be better if she were to disappear. He said it was a nice summer night and the lake would be calm. Hsu-shen lined up a boat north of Waukegan. They would take the woman, put her in the trunk and drive up to the boat. Drive ten miles out on Lake Michigan, tie some chains around her feet, and throw her overboard.

Hsu-shen agreed with Wong. It would make a better headline. *Shady Woman Linked to Chinese Gangster Disappears.* The racist *gwai los* would think she had it coming, fooling around with a Chinaman.

Maitland said, "Do you have plans tonight?"

"No," Bianca said. "Max is working."

"Would you like to have some coffee?" They did this sometimes after work. Neither one of them took it to mean anything.

Bianca said, "Not tonight, uh? I'm pretty tired."

"All right." Maitland said, "You're okay, then?"

"I'm fine, Evan."

She was giving him a look now, a sort of half-smile, telling him she didn't want to be mothered. They had kept their discussions to work today. Maitland telling her he could go to Philadelphia for the auction if she didn't feel like going, Bianca saying that she

would still be going, she hadn't been trau-
matized for Christ's sake. Then Maitland
raising his palm, saying she could have it
her way.

Then feeling relieved that she would be
going out of town. Not that he wouldn't
miss her, because he would, because it
would be good for her to get out of Chicago
for a while. They stepped around the things
that would set off arguments or too much
personal dialogue. Maitland did not discuss
Julie's accusations and did not ask any more
questions about Bianca's failure to get a
gun. Bianca would have said, what good
would it do? Substituting drama for discussion.

It made things uneasy for both of them.
Different worldviews on a personal crisis.
One of them thinking that there really was
no crisis to begin with, the other one being
Maitland. Their friendship was solid, perhaps even intimate. But she could rankle
him at times by telling him he had been a
policeman too long. It was her trump card.
A simple way of summing up his cynicism
or his paranoia or his politics. It pissed him
off sometimes.

Now she said, "Do you mind locking up
tonight?"

"No."

"Okay." She reached for her bag. "Good-night, Evan." Then she was walking toward the front door.

He walked behind her and locked the door after her. He was walking back to the office when he looked out the window and saw a car go by. Moving enough that he could not really see who or what was inside. But he looked again when it made a sudden U-turn and passed by the window again. Then it was gone, out of his sight.

A car making a U-turn, three men inside. Asian . . . ?

— what?

Paranoia . . . so be it, he thought as he walked to the front door. Bianca's car would be parked down the street. He couldn't see it from inside the shop. He hurried as he took his keys out of his pocket and unlocked the door, hoping it *was* his own paranoia working on him now, better to be crazy and anxious than sorry, getting the door un-locked and stepping outside and looking down the street.

Christ.

A Chrysler parked alongside Bianca's Mercedes, a big Chinese lifting her off the ground and putting her in the open trunk of the Chrysler, a smaller man standing next to him.

"Hey!" Maitland yelled and started running toward them. And the big one shut the trunk and cut off Bianca's screams. The smaller one next to the driver's side said something to the big one and the big one got in the back as the smaller one reached into the car and came out with a pistol and started firing at Maitland.

Maitland jumped behind a parked car. He was unarmed and all they would have to do was walk down to where he was and shoot him and that would be the end of it, but they didn't, the smaller one got in the car and Maitland heard them drive off.

Maitland ran across the street to his own car and before he could get in the Chrysler had already turned the corner. Maitland started the BMW and shoved it in gear and squealed off after them.

Maitland felt a horror, a shock. He had just talked to her. He had just said goodnight to her. He had not offered to walk her to her car. Had not even thought about it. But these thoughts were fleeting and soon replaced by a cold rage. Taking her and putting her in a trunk . . .

Po-han was driving quickly. Hsu-shen was concerned about having him floor it because he didn't want to attract any police with an abducted woman in the trunk. He said to Big Kon, "Who was that?"

"I don't know. Just some guy."

Hsu-shen was looking out the back window. They were in a fair amount of traffic now, not far from Evanston. Some fool wanting to be heroic and save a woman. Had he called the police? Had he seen their license plate?

Hsu-shen said to Po-han, "Take it easy. We don't want to get pulled over."

Maitland looked down at the passenger seat, hoping his cell phone would materialize there. It didn't. It was back in the shop. He could not call the police. If he pulled over to stop at a pay phone, he would lose sight of the Chrysler. Bianca would be gone, almost certainly murdered by these fucking animals. The sight of her being lifted into the trunk of the car still with him . . .

They were on this road, ahead of him, weren't they? He could see taillights that were familiar a block or so ahead, but it could be a different car altogether. Not night yet, but getting darker and it wasn't so easy to see things in the distance. It could be the wrong car and if he followed the wrong one she would die, he would be responsible for letting her die. Didn't walk her to her car, didn't even offer . . .

The traffic light turned yellow and then it was red and cars ahead of him stopped, and he pulled out into the oncoming lane and floored it, shooting out into the intersection and there was a truck on his left and he had to swerve back hard to avoid it, the truck's horn blaring at him.

And then he was on the next block, hammering the accelerator again. And the car was another block ahead, going through the next intersection and Maitland remembered that they had turned the corner before he had gotten into his car. They wouldn't know his car, wouldn't know he was in it unless he got too close and it was an advantage, it had to be, because if he caught up with them, he wouldn't be able to slam the car into them because it might get Bianca killed, but she was in the trunk and they were in the cabin and at least they were separated from her, but she was still their hostage.

There were two cars in front of him, blocking his path and Maitland laid on the horn and hit the brights and finally one of them moved forward and over and gave him the lane and Maitland floored it ahead and then was switching lanes here and there, getting past cars going much slower than he and now the Chrysler was in sight, getting in a lane that merged onto Highway 41, going north.

Maitland took the same road, but there was a lot of traffic and now the Chrysler was moving faster, getting up to fifty or sixty miles per hour and the cars and the trucks impeded Maitland's ability to catch up with them. And then Maitland noted a slowing in the traffic, a stoplight up ahead. The vehicles ahead of him slowing even more and there were so many of them there was no getting around. And then the traffic slowed even more, and then it stopped.

Maitland put the gear in park and got out of the car.

He ran between stopped cars, the road curving, people sitting in their stationary vehicles watching a rather ordinary-looking man wearing slacks and a jacket running up the aisle, thinking he was insane. He ran past SUVs with soccer moms behind the wheels, commuters listening to NPR and satellite radios and the local traffic reports from helicopters buzzing over Chicagoland traffic. He ran about eighty yards and he saw the Chrysler and the light up ahead turned green and he saw the brake lights on the back of the Chrysler go off and he knew it was moving ahead now and he would never catch it.

So he suppressed a cry and turned around and ran back toward the BMW, cars moving past him now in the opposite direction and he saw his BMW sitting and cars pulling out around it, some of them honking in anger at the empty vehicle as if it could move on its own, and Maitland reached it and got inside and put it in drive and roared forward.

The men in the Chrysler were unaware that they were being pursued. But Hsu-shen did not feel like relaxing. He was familiar with this stretch of road. You could take it almost all the way into Wisconsin, the lake on your right. But there were traffic lights about every mile and it could wear your patience down. He turned to Po-han and said, "Take a left at the next intersection and get on the interstate."

Maitland tried to push his way closer to the Chrysler, but traffic was tight and more than once he had to honk his horn to get people to let him move left or right. Bursts of acceleration followed by heavy braking to avoid smacking into someone from behind, and it was a hard thing keeping himself from boiling over. He kept one hand on the wheel as he reached over and opened up his glove compartment. The Glock .45 was there and he knew it was loaded. Using two hands he racked the slide and put a bullet in the chamber and he concentrated on the road again, seeing an opening that he grabbed and he succeeded in putting another five cars behind him.

And then traffic was slowing again and he knew they were coming to another stoplight. Maitland slowed the car. He had no choice. And his heart was racing as the traffic slowed even more, then came to a full stop.

Maitland got out. He stuffed the .45 into his belt and started running again.

Three lanes of traffic, sitting as if in a parking lot, but their engines were running and if the light turned green and they started moving forward, he would be fucked, but it wasn't time to be thinking that now, the Chrysler would have to be behind the light, somewhere among this mass of vehicles and his side was hurting now and his breathing was labored and he could hear people honking at him, but it didn't matter because about forty yards up ahead was the Chrysler, sitting in traffic, waiting like the rest of them, three men inside the car and Maitland knew it was them.

He slowed himself to a trot and then to a walk as he got closer to the car and he saw movement inside. The man in the passenger seat in the front must have seen him in the rearview mirror. It was the man who had shot at him and Maitland couldn't hear what they were saying, but then the big one in the back turned around and looked at him through the back window. The big one opened the door and got out, Maitland walking toward him.

Maitland took the .45 out of his belt and shot him twice in the chest. The big man went to the ground and Maitland heard shouts from the car and Maitland used two hands as he took stance and aimed and shot the driver in the back of the head.

Po-han died before he could get the car in gear. Hsu-shen was reaching for the pistol on the car seat, but now Maitland was aiming for him too and another shot came through the back window and Hsu-shen opened the door and let himself fall out onto the road. Two more shots as Hsu-shen scrambled away between cars on his right, his gun still in the car and he was up and running.

Maitland saw him escape from the car and

then the man was amidst other cars and it would be too risky to take a shot then, have a stray one go in someone else's windshield. The man was running and then he was gone.

Maitland lowered his gun.

He walked past Big Kon's body and to the driver's seat. Pushed Po-han over and reached in to turn the ignition off. There was blood and bits of the driver's head on the steering wheel and some had landed on the keys as well. Maitland didn't notice it. He took the keys and walked back to the trunk and opened it to let his friend out.

He got her to her feet and said, "Are you all right?"

She embraced him, murmuring answers. And they stood there holding each other up in traffic.

Twenty-Two

Sam Stillman was not a big man. Five foot seven on a good day, wearing suspenders and a tie over a starched white shirt. He had that sort of prominent, overly large head that you sometimes see on actors and high-profile trial lawyers. Lest anyone be unaware of his profession, he drove a loud white Corvette that said "DEFENDER" on the license tag. He liked the spotlight, liked being on television, liked being center stage. And like many successful trial lawyers, he liked a good fight.

Maitland had called him shortly after the first set of police officers arrived at the scene. He surrendered his gun to them and said he would explain it all. That wasn't good enough, they said, and they were soon yelling at both of them until Maitland lawyered up and within an hour he and Bianca were sitting in an interrogation room with Sam and a couple of North Chicago detectives and an assistant district attorney who was a year shy of thirty and had heard all about Sam Stillman.

Sam spoke to her first, reeling off names of the people he had worked with when he was Deputy D.A. himself, asking her how they were doing, laughing, smiling, telling her he remembered his early days as an A.D.A., and in general speaking to her as a veteran would to a first-year rookie, and even if she was aware that she was being patronized, it didn't matter because within a few minutes, he had her psyched into thinking she was merely a guest at this event, but being a man of generosity and good heart, he was going to help her get through it.

The detectives sensed this and now had something else to be angry about. Two dead men on a highway in the middle of the evening traffic and the Chicago Police Department was not going to tolerate reckless vigilantes.

Sam Stillman said, "Gentlemen, let's get some things clear, okay? First of all, my client has a license to carry that gun and use it when necessary. The law states that one may use deadly force to prevent death or serious bodily harm to oneself *and to others*. Now you know that as well as I do."

One of the detectives said, "There are witnesses who say those men were unarmed."

Sam Stillman said, "Were there or were there not weapons found in that car? Yes, there were. Did they or did they not fire on Mr. Maitland outside his store? Yes, they did."

"We cannot condone citizens taking the law into their own hands. He could have called the police."

"When?" Sam said. "He left his cell phone in the store. It all happened very quickly. Now I know how you fellows hate being second guessed after being in situations like this. And I don't blame you for feeling that way. Yours is one of the hardest jobs there is. Now can you give this man the same consideration?"

"We're police officers." The detective turned to Maitland and said, "Tell me this: how did you know it was the same men on the road that were in front of your store?"

Sam said to Maitland, "Don't answer that." He said to the detective, "Why are you even asking something like that? You know the answer already."

"I —"

"Ms. Garibaldi was in the trunk. The question is moot."

"But she may not have been."

"What . . . what the hell are you talking about?" Sam said. "She *was*. Are you wanting to arrest this man based on alternative possibilities?"

"Mr. Stillman?"

It was the assistant D.A. speaking now.

"Yes?" Sam said. His voice was solicitous. A law professor taking a question from one of his students.

"Mr. Stillman," she said. "The concern is the danger to the other people around. Someone else could have been hurt."

"But they weren't. Mr. Maitland let a third man get away because he didn't want to risk hurting an innocent bystander." Sam Stillman smiled. "Gentlemen, I have to say I don't understand this. If one of your officers had done this, you would have awarded him the medal of valor. He does it and you want to find some reason to arrest him? I don't understand."

Maitland said, "He's still out there."

"Excuse me?" one of the detectives said.

"Evan," Sam said, trying to discourage him from talking.

"He's still out there," Maitland said. "The guy that shot at me. The one who probably was in charge of this abduction. My question is, what are you doing about getting him?"

"Evan —"

The detective Maitland was glaring at was trying to give it back. He said, "We're working on it."

"Are you?" Maitland said. "You seem more interested in trying to pin something on me. Not that I give a shit. But as far as I'm concerned, she's still in danger."

"Evan, don't —"

The detective said, "We're handling it. Why don't you let us instead of going apeshit in public places with your fucking registered gun?"

Maitland shook his head. He had once been one of these guys, but it was still difficult to understand them. He sighed, feeling very tired now. He said, "Don't you see? They were going to kill her."

He said it aware that Bianca was sitting next to him. But he saw no point in her not knowing that. She probably knew already.

The detective said, "You don't know that."

Maitland wanted to hit him then. Reach across the table, grab his tie, pull him close, and just slug him. The stupid son of a bitch. A woman's life at stake and this guy wanted to win a pissing contest with an ex-cop. How did assholes like this make detective?

Sam Stillman said, "Evan, will you please stop talking?"

■ ■ ■ ■

Later they were in the parking lot. Sam Still-man walked Maitland and Bianca to Mait-land's car. Sam asked Bianca if he could speak with Maitland alone for a minute and she said that was fine.

Maitland had heard about Sam Stillman before he met him. A rich, cocky defense lawyer who liked high-profile cases. Sam had represented a man named Thomas Hicks who was charged with two counts of homicide after killing two gangsters who were gunning for him. Hicks made bail, in part because of a personal guarantee made by Sam Stillman. Then Hicks jumped bail and Maitland was hired to bring him back. Maitland turned out to be wrong about Thomas Hicks, a man who was basically all right and had legitimately acted in self-defense.

Maitland realized that, in a way, he was wrong about Sam Stillman too. Like most cops, Maitland didn't like lawyers until he needed one. Through his experience with the Hicks job, Maitland came to see that Sam Stillman was conscientious and ethical in addition to being smart.

Now Sam said, "Aren't you glad you

called me?"

Maitland smiled, in spite of it all. He said, "Sorry if I embarrassed you, speaking out of turn."

Sam Stillman waved it off. "Forget it," he said. "I tell you, I've seen a lot in my career, but I can never quite understand why it is cops go after other cops."

"I'm not a cop anymore."

"Yeah, but you were. You'd think there would be some sort of professional courtesy."

"Is there in your business?"

"More often than not," Sam said. He almost sounded defensive. Sam Stillman liked to tell people that law was an honorable profession, even if some of its practitioners weren't.

Sam said, "Well, I can't say for sure, but I don't think they're going to file charges on you."

"She tell you that?" Maitland was referring to the young prosecutor.

"It's not really up to her," Sam Stillman said. "The detectives will push her, but the D.A. will resist it. I told them that I'd make it painful for them. Tell the media and the court that they're trying to make you a scapegoat because of their own inability to find out who killed that guy in Hyde Park."

"That's what I've been saying."

"Yeah, but it's different when I say it." Sam smiled. "Evan?"

"Yeah."

"Did you really leave your cell phone in the store?"

"Of course." Maitland looked at the lawyer. He said, "Et tu, Brute?"

Sam Stillman raised his hand. "I don't judge, buddy. I just defend. But be careful, huh?"

TWENTY-THREE

In the car, Maitland said, "You called your husband, didn't you?"

She looked over at him for a moment before answering. Then said, "I didn't, actually."

Maitland said, "You didn't?"

"He . . . he's working tonight. And things happened so quickly. Going to the police station, all that."

Yeah, it was a whirlwind, Maitland thought. *But you get abducted and almost killed and you don't call your husband.* He said, "I don't understand."

"You're not married."

"I know that, but . . ."

"Evan, what would I have told him?"

Maitland said, "You would have told him what happened, that you were okay now and . . . I don't know, you tell him."

"And then he says, well, thank God you're okay and we go back to our life?"

She was smiling at him now, the way a teacher smiles at a kid who's not quite getting it.

Maitland said, "I don't know what he'll say."

She shook her head. "No, you don't. He'll want me to say that everything's okay and that we continue as if there's nothing wrong. And if I tell him that it's not okay, that there are people out there who are hunting me, he won't want to hear that. He'll get angry."

"Angry? Why?"

"I don't know. Maybe because he's afraid. Maybe because he feels helpless." Bianca shrugged. "It's not his fault."

"Well, no one's saying it's his fault. I don't get this."

"It's private, Evan. I've already said too much."

After a moment, Maitland said, "All right." And let the conversation drop.

They drove through the Wilmette village, quiet and sleepy and white bread. It was cozy and nice. Expensive North Shore real estate a forty-minute train ride from downtown, but it was an illusion of comfort and safety. Men knew who she was and where she worked and it was a safe bet that they knew where she lived too. She had been targeted.

Bianca's house was a two-story taupe brick located on a tree-lined street. A tony neighborhood just a few blocks from Lake Michigan. There was a Lexus in the driveway.

Bianca said, "Max is home."

She turned to Maitland and for a moment his heart jumped.

It had happened a couple of times since he had known her. A man and a woman can know each other, sometimes even for years, and not feel an impulse, but moments and body language can speak more effectively than we know. And in that moment, he felt that she wanted to kiss him. He would have liked that.

Bianca was looking at him.

But Maitland thought, it isn't fair. Not after what she's been through. She's not drunk, she's not under the influence of a drug. But after what she's been through, she couldn't be in her right mind.

Maitland said, "Listen."

"Yes?"

"I'd like to talk to your husband."

"Now?"

"Yes. Let me go in there with you and tell him what happened."

Bianca frowned. "I don't think that's a

good idea."

"I'm not trying to interfere," Maitland said. "Just let me talk to him. Please."

"Okay."

Maitland cut the ignition and shut off the car. He followed Bianca to the door and she unlocked it and they went inside.

Max Sanderson was a tall, handsome man. Gray haired and looking a bit like Richard Gere. He was in his fifties.

Maitland had thought Max might be gay the first time he met him. But Maitland allowed that his own background may have played into this. Maitland's upbringing had been working class and his subsequent career in police work brought him little contact with people like Max Sanderson. Max Sanderson was always nice, always polite, but Maitland thought his aloof, aristocratic air was something of an affectation. As if he had decided that this was the person he wanted to appear to be and then he worked to become that person. When Max spoke, Maitland was sometimes reminded of an NPR host.

Still, Maitland was also aware that he was simply jealous of the man. He was Bianca's husband and Maitland wanted to find flaws in him.

Bianca called out his name and he came out of the kitchen. He was holding a glass of wine. Pleasant greetings were exchanged. Max asked Maitland if he wanted a drink. Maitland said no thanks and then hesitated a moment before saying, "I need to tell you what happened."

After they had told him, Max said, "I don't understand this. Why aren't there police parked out front?"

"You mean guarding you?" Maitland said.

"Protecting us," Max said. "These guys are after her."

Maitland said, "They've gotten in touch with Wilmette PD. They'll patrol your house here and there."

"Here and there?"

"And the store as well."

Max said, "That's it? And what about in between? What about when she's not at work or not here?"

"I don't know," Maitland said. "There's only so much they can do. I'm loaning her a gun. A .38 revolver, it's fairly compact and easy to use. It was in the trunk of my car. She can carry it in her purse."

Max said, ". . . a gun? Those are illegal."

"It's illegal to own one in the city. Not out here."

Max Sanderson looked to his wife, uneasy. He could see that it had already been discussed between her and Evan. He said, "I don't know . . ."

Maitland said, "It's not a lifestyle change, Max. It'll just be until this thing settles."

"And when will that be?"

"When they find this man. The one behind this and arrest him. Or kill him."

Max was shaking his head now. He said, "I don't like this."

"It's not for you to like," Maitland said, his patience being tested now. He said, "Look, it's happened and it's not her fault or yours. It just is."

Max said, "For you, this may be a way of life. It's not for us."

"I'm aware of that. But sometimes it chooses you whether you like it or not."

"Really?" Max said, giving Maitland a superior look now. Max said, "I can't help thinking that you brought this on."

Bianca said, "Max —"

Maitland said, "What?" He was knocked back, not having seen this coming.

"You heard me," Max said. "We were doing fine. No drama, no crime, no issues here until you came into her life."

"Max," Bianca said, "don't be stupid."

"You're attracted to violence. And now

you've brought her into this."

Bianca said, "Max, shut up."

Max ignored his wife, saying to Maitland, "It's what you wanted all along, isn't it? To bring her in."

"*Max, stop it.* Just be quiet, please."

Max said to Maitland, "Are you happy now?"

Maitland sighed and got to his feet. He stepped away from Max, his body language retreating.

Maitland almost said, "You're drunk." But he didn't. Instead he said, "You're upset. We can discuss this some other time. I'll see myself out. But if you need anything, call me."

Bianca gave her husband a glare then caught up with Maitland at the front door.

"I'm sorry," she said.

"Forget it," Maitland said. "You have a burglar alarm?"

"Yes."

"And the gun in your purse."

"Yes."

"If the time comes, you'll have to use it, you know."

"I know," she said. "Evan, he's wrong about you. Please, *please* don't take what he said seriously."

"I don't. He's . . ." Maitland stopped himself.

Bianca said, "I know what he is. He's not like that when he's sober. He's not."

"I'm sure he isn't," Maitland said. "Goodnight, Bianca."

Max was still sitting on the couch, his wineglass refilled. And at the moment Bianca truly disliked him. Didn't hate him, but had contempt for him. A stranger before her, a chemical being.

He looked at her and said, "Did you patch it up with him?" He thought he was being clever.

Bianca said, "You know, I should videotape you when you're like this. Play it back for you the next day, see how you like it."

"Like what? Oh, I've embarrassed you."

"You're drunk. And when you drink too much, you do stupid shit like this. Do you understand what he did?"

"What did he do?"

"He saved my life. And you didn't even fucking thank him. I can't comprehend it."

"So I have embarrassed you."

"Jesus Christ. Do you resent him for it?"

"For what? Saving you? Mister macho shithead, coming to your rescue?"

"He's not like that. You don't know him."

"Are you in love with him?"

"Oh, Jesus. I've worked with him for several years. Have I ever given you any reason, any reason, to think I've been unfaithful to you?"

"I don't know. Have you?"

"For God's sake. Have I let you down in some way? Do you blame me for your drinking?"

"Oh, stop with the drama. I don't have a problem. There is no one to blame. We're having a discussion here and you want to turn it into alcoholism. For all I know, you're doing that to hide something you're doing. Or feeling."

"I can't talk to you when you're like this," she said. "I'm going to bed."

TWENTY-FOUR

The car pulled to a stop on lower Wacker
Drive. Wong got out and one of his bodyguards got out with him. The other bodyguards remained in the car. Boats cruised
slowly down the Chicago River, their prows
slushing the water aside. Wong crossed the
street and walked down the steps by the
Michigan Avenue bridge.

Wong liked Chicago at night. A clean city
with good, solid American architecture. For
the Americans, it was a big city. Though
nothing to match the populations of Hong
Kong or Beijing. Wong liked this at times,
other times he did not. Events could happen in Beijing and simply merge into the
vast crowds. No television coverage or worries because those things were controlled by
the State. It was easier to hide crime in a
city of thirteen million.

Wong watched the boat with the summer
tourists pass by, some of them taking photos

of the Sheraton Hotel before they got to the Wrigley Building.

Hsu-shen walked toward him. Then he was standing there. Alone.

Wong made a gesture to his bodyguard and the man walked off so that Wong could be alone with Hsu-shen.

Wong kept his eyes on the river when he first spoke. He said, "My wife wants me to hire a public relations firm."

Hsu-shen did not respond.

Wong said, "She says in America, it is necessary to do such things. If you're going to be in the public eye."

"Yes?" Hsu-shen said.

"Do you know what it costs to have one on retainer?"

"No."

"About half a million dollars. Just to start. Perhaps it is a scheme. I told her I'd think about it."

Hsu-shen said nothing.

And Wong said, "You didn't succeed, did you?"

"No. Big Kon is dead. Po-han too."

"How?"

"We took her as she came out of her shop. She was alone. But a man came out after her."

"A policeman?"

"I'm not sure. He didn't look like one. But I'll find out who he is. I shot at him, but he . . . he got away. We took off and he came after us."

"Caught you."

"Yes. He caught up with us. He was armed. He shot Big Kon and Po-han before I knew what was happening."

"And you?"

"I escaped."

"Leaving the woman with him."

"He was armed. I couldn't get close to him."

"Who is he?"

"I don't know. He might have been a cop. He might have been a bodyguard. I didn't know, Preston."

"You didn't know he would be there."

"No. I didn't know."

"Did he see you?"

"He shot at me. Whether or not he'd recognized me, I don't know. I had to get out of there before the police arrived."

"I understand that," Wong said. "Well, I can get you out of town if necessary. Hide you in San Francisco's Chinatown and it would be very hard for the police to find you there. But then Wu would want to know why I'm doing that. Do you see the problem?"

"Yes, boss."

"I am not afraid, Hsu-shen. I am confident you will take care of it. This time, however, you'll know about this other man. Won't you?"

"I haven't forgotten him," Hsu-shen said.

Wong said, "Do it soon." He walked off to the stairs.

TWENTY-FIVE

It was about eleven when Maitland got back to the city. He was driving down Lake Shore Drive, his window rolled down to bring in the cool air off the water. He peeled the car off at the Belmont exit and that was when his cell phone rang.

"Evan?"

It was Julie.

"Hey," he said.

She said, "Where are you?"

"I'm close to my apartment. I just got back from Wilmette."

Julie said, "Where Bianca lives."

"Yes. Have you —"

"Yeah, I heard about it."

"Who told you?"

"Well, let's see. It was on the nine o'clock news to begin with." Her voice was tight, controlled. She said, "Can you meet me?"

"Sure. At the apartment?"

"No. I'm on shift tonight. Don't ask why.

235

The stand?"

"I should be there in about five."

The Cubs game had ended an hour or so before, but people were still milling around, not wanting to go home. The blue and white kiosk across the street from Wrigley Field was still open. Maitland got there first and bought a bottle of water and some peanuts. He stood there eating the peanuts and drinking the water as he looked down on a stack of newspapers. He decided the peanuts weren't going to make much of a dinner and he asked the guy if he had any hot dogs left. He said he did and Maitland asked for two.

He was paying for them when an unmarked Crown Victoria pulled up. Julie got out and said something to the other cop behind the wheel. Probably to come back in five minutes or ten, but it wouldn't take her too long. The car pulled away and she started walking toward him.

Oh, looking a little angry too.

Got to him and said, "What the hell do you think you're doing?"

"What?"

"Killing two people on a highway? Two men that may not have even been armed?"

Maitland said, "I think you've been misin-

236

formed."

"They're talking about charging you."

"Let 'em."

"Oh, okay. Let them. That's real smart, Evan. Really smart."

"They haven't got anything on me and they know it. Besides, you'd've done the same thing. In fact, you have. For me."

He was referring to the time she had saved his life in Wisconsin. Men surrounding him with guns, making him dig his own grave, and the first shot fired was by her, hiding in the woods.

"You bastard," she said. "You're going to use that against me?"

"I'm not using it against you. You did nothing wrong then. And I'm never going to forget that you did it."

"Those men were going to kill you. They had guns pointed at you."

"So did these guys."

"That's not what I heard," she said.

There was a silence between them. She had taken someone's side on this and it wasn't his.

In a voice that was more subdued, Maitland said, "Well, I don't know what you heard."

"Oh, shit, Evan. I'm on your side, don't you know that? But can you try, at least try, to see it from my perspective?"

Maitland said, "I don't follow you."

Julie said nothing.

And Maitland said, "Oh. You weren't just told about this, were you? I mean, someone spoke to you, didn't they?"

"I . . ."

"Your supervisor, perhaps? Or was it a friendly co-worker? Someone who meant well?"

"It doesn't matter who it was."

Maitland sighed. He said, "Maybe it doesn't. But you were advised, maybe warned, that it wasn't good for your career to be associating with someone like me. Is that about right?"

"Yeah," she said, "that's about the size of it." She was looking away from him now.

For a while, neither one of them said anything. Traffic passed by in the street. Kids still buzzing off the ballpark beers and excitement of the game, the night still young for them.

Maitland said, "Julie."

"Yes?"

"They're probably right."

Julie said, "But that's not what I'm . . . I'm not a careerist, Evan. I'm not."

"I know you're not."

"I'm not even sure I want to be a sergeant."

"If you did," Maitland said slowly. "If you did, I don't think that would be a bad thing."

She looked at him.

"You deserve it, Julie."

She said, "I didn't come here to do this. I didn't come here to give you an ultimatum."

"You haven't."

She was not one to cry. Not her. But there was pain and a different sort of anger on her face now. She said, "Is that what you want?"

"Oh, shit. It doesn't matter what I want. We're not kids, Julie. We're up against a, well I don't know what to call it. I'm not worth ruining your career over. I'm just not."

"Do you love me?"

"Yes. I always have. But that doesn't solve this."

"Maybe it would. Maybe if you would . . . give me something . . . more."

Maitland said, "I don't think that's a good idea. I don't think it's what you want either."

Julie said, "Well. It seems clear that it's not what you want."

The Crown Vic had come back.

Julie said, "Those things you said to me

when you called me from Kansas . . . that you wanted me at home waiting for you. That was a lie?"

Oh, shit. Kansas. He had called her after a night of violence and fear that he wouldn't live to see the sun come up. Fear that he would die in some far-off prairie. He thought that he would never see her again.

But she hadn't been all he thought of and he had known it even then. But he didn't think he had misled her.

He said now, "No. I meant them."

"Right," she said. Looking away from him now. "I gotta go," she said.

Maitland watched her get in the Crown Vic and watched it drive away.

Maitland parked the BMW in the garage next to the Pontiac. He shut the door behind it and walked up the fire escape stairs. He unlocked his back door and let himself in. He was wondering if Julie would come get her things tomorrow or if she would wait a few days. He wondered how long it would take for the scent of her perfume to drift out. He wondered if she was ashamed of him. He wondered if he would care if she was. He wondered if she hated him and decided he wouldn't like it much if she did.

He took off his jacket. He placed his gun on the kitchen counter and walked into the bathroom to wash his face. Turned on the taps to get the temperature he wanted as he rolled up the sleeves to his shirt.

After he dried his face, he looked at his watch. Not quite midnight. Maybe he could see himself on the news, hear the Chicago PD say mean things about him. Never mind the victim.

Then he looked at the counter and saw that his gun was no longer there.

He turned to see a Chinese man now sitting in his living room chair. Pointing a Browning semiautomatic at him.

"I put it away," Frank Chang said. "I think there's been enough shooting for the day."

Twenty-Six

Maitland looked at him for quite a while before he said anything. Chinese guy wearing a dark suit, but not the one that had taken a shot at him in front of the antique store. But Chinese and they were the ones misbehaving these last couple of days.

Maitland nodded toward this one's Browning. He said, "You sure?"

Frank Chang said, "We need to talk. I find it easier to talk with this."

"I see," Maitland said. "What do we have to talk about?"

Frank said, "You killed two men today."

"That's right."

"Why?"

"They had abducted a friend of mine. They were going to kill her."

"Right. Why don't you sit down?"

"Why?"

"I told you. We need to talk."

Maitland gestured to the refrigerator.

"Can I get a drink first?"

"No."

"Why not?"

"Because you keep a gun in the refrigerator."

"I think you're paranoid."

"No. I found it. A little .38, titanium lightweight. Not much good in distance or at night, but helpful for protection in home invasion."

Maitland said, "The man knows his guns. I guess you hid that too."

"Yes. I hid the sawed-off shotgun too. The one you keep under the bed."

"Well, then can I get a drink?"

"No. Sit down, please."

Maitland took a seat on the couch, the barrel of the man's Browning following him as he did so. The man was smooth. Probably a professional . . . very likely a professional. He had gotten into the apartment and left no signs of a break-in.

Frank said, "So. You are a furniture salesman?"

"Yes."

"A criminal as well?"

"No. It's a legitimate business."

Frank said, "Why the firearms?"

"You a cop?"

"No. Why the firearms?"

"I like to be careful. Chicago's a tough city."

"Is it." Frank frowned. "Are you a professional bodyguard?"

"No."

"Military?"

"No."

"What are you then?"

"Like you said. A furniture salesman."

Frank Chang smiled. He said, "I saw the news while I was having dinner at a bar. What you did, north of the city. That's not what salesmen do. That's what criminals do."

"Yeah," Maitland said. "The police seem to share that viewpoint."

Frank Chang studied this man for a moment. He said, "You used to be a policeman, didn't you?"

"Some time ago."

"I see," Frank said. "The woman. Is she your wife, your girlfriend?"

"She's my friend. My business partner."

"Hmmm." Frank was studying Maitland again. Then he said, "Is she all right?"

"What do you care?"

"I'm just asking. Did they injure her? That's all."

"If you're wanting to know where she is, you're wasting your time. She's in police custody. They've got her guarded several times over."

"The police do?"

"Yes."

"Do you know where?"

"They didn't tell me. They're rather put out with me, in fact."

"For what? Killing those men?"

"Yes."

"Yes. A vigilante, huh?"

"That's what they think."

"Yes," Frank said. "And they're right to think so. But what does it matter what they think?"

Maitland said, "You weren't in the car, were you?"

"No. The one that got away from you, his name is Hsu-shen."

"You know him?"

"Yes. I know him."

"A friend?"

"No."

"You working with him?"

"No."

"You working *for* him?"

"No."

"What do you want with me then?"

"I want to know what the woman was doing there."

"Doing where?"

"At Raymond Liu's apartment. What was she doing there?"

"She was just doing business with him, that's all. He had . . . access to some sort of Chinese antiques that we needed."

"Was she involved in his other businesses?"

"No."

"Were you?"

"No. What is it you're talking about? Money laundering, that sort of thing?"

"Yes."

"We don't do that. I know you may not believe me because of the guns and . . . whatever. But we're not drug dealers, either one of us. We've never been in the money laundering business. We've never worked with Raymond Liu in any capacity. The woman is a civilian. I swear."

"Okay," Frank said. "That's what I thought."

Maitland regarded the Chinese. Then said, "Oh, my God. You're the guy that let her go, aren't you?"

Frank said nothing.

Maitland said, "You're an assassin."

Frank still said nothing.

Maitland said, "You were sent there to kill Liu?"

"Yes."

"By Hsu-shen?"

"No. Not directly."

Maitland said, "I read somewhere that the Chinese triads usually bring their assassins in from out of town."

"Sometimes."

"What about you?"

"Chicago is not my home."

"Fair enough. You came here for Raymond Liu. Were you involved in that thing at Ravinia's too?"

Frank shrugged.

Maitland said, "A DEA agent was killed. A policeman."

Frank Chang said, "We did not intend that."

Maitland said, "They say that the man killed at Ravinia's was a heroin chemist. The A number one chemist for the Red Lantern Triad. Is that true?"

"Yes."

"And what about Liu?"

"What about him?"

"Was he in the Red Lantern too?"

"Yes. A money launderer. I thought that would be apparent to someone like you."

"Well, it wasn't. If I had known, I would have prevented her from meeting with him."

"But you didn't. And she did."

Maitland was tensing up. The man was

right and the man was holding a gun, but it couldn't prevent him from feeling angry. The man was judging him. Maybe even calling him a fool.

Maitland said, "Okay, maybe I dropped the ball there. But that's my problem."

"No," Frank said. "It's her problem. You think you did something heroic this evening. You think you saved her life. But all you did was give her another day, maybe a few more days of life. They'll come after her again. And you're not always going to be there for her. You're not now."

Maitland flushed. "She's married. She's married to someone else. What am I supposed to do?"

"She can leave the city. Set up business someplace else."

Maitland said, "Is that what you're here for? To tell me to get her out of town? Is this your mission of benevolence?"

"No. I'm not here for them. I don't work for them."

"You don't work for who?"

"I don't work for the Wu-Chai Triad." Frank said, "They're the ones that brought me in. Do you know Preston Wong?"

"I know of him."

"He's their deputy *shan chu*. That's Chinese for 'master.' He runs the Chicago branch of the Wu-Chai Triad."

"Where are they based?"

"San Francisco."

Maitland said, "And trying to wrest control from this other triad, the Red Lantern?"

"Yes."

"The heroin trade? Is that what this dispute is about?"

Frank said, "Heroin, yes. But that's just the means. It's money, power. The usual things."

"But what does Bianca have to do with this?"

"Well, after talking to you, it seems she has nothing to do with it. But they want her dead now."

"Because she saw you?"

"I doubt that. She must have seen someone else. Or saw something else." Frank Chang made a gesture. "It doesn't much matter."

"It doesn't matter? She hasn't done anything."

"She's a witness. That's enough."

"But . . . Preston Wong. He's in the newspaper, he's a public figure."

Frank said, "In Taipei, he was a policeman. He worked for the Wu-Chai then."

"He was a policeman? You mean he was an inside man?"

"In China, the police and the triads sometimes work together."

"But we're talking about murdering an innocent civilian."

"He already has. He is in charge. Mr. Maitland, you think this is barbaric?"

"Yes."

"But you are not Chinese. You don't understand. Wong wants to take over the heroin trade. He has spent time and money investing in this community. He's made himself protected through political contacts and with his money. This is how it works. Your friend is a threat to that so long as she is alive. She is a threat to him, to the Wu-Chai and, perhaps most importantly, to the well-being of his family."

"But she hasn't done anything."

"You're not listening to me. *That doesn't matter.* He cannot lose everything because of some woman he doesn't even know. For Wong, the question is not whether or not she deserves to die. The question is, can he allow her to live when it threatens the well-being of his family? He knows the answer."

"Is that what you're here for? To explain it to me?"

"I'm here to let you know what you're dealing with."

"Well, thanks for the help," Maitland said,

his anger still there. "But I'm having trouble believing that your motive is one of generosity."

"It isn't."

"Then what do you want?"

"The Wu-Chai betrayed me. They tried to have me killed after the Liu contract. But I survived that."

"Bianca said there was another man there. She said you shot him."

"I did. He was trying to kill me. But I had seen it coming."

"Why don't you leave town then?"

"Because they haven't paid me what they owe me."

"I see," Maitland said. "And you feel . . . dishonored by this?"

Frank Chang said, "Perhaps."

"Isn't it funny how often honor and principle come into play when someone owes you money?"

"Yes. Very funny," Frank said. "But the money isn't all of it. When they set me up for this, they were saying something about me. Perhaps they were saying something about my own family. An insult, perhaps. I can go home, but I risk losing face if I go home with nothing. I don't ask you to understand it."

"Good. Because I don't. Besides, it seems

pretty clear you want something from me now."

"Perhaps," Frank said.

"Well," Maitland said, "I can tell you right now I'm not going to kill Preston Wong for you. Or help you do it."

"If you don't, he'll kill your woman."

She's not my woman, Maitland thought. But he said, "That's what you say. You could be selling me a line of shit."

"I could be. But I'm not."

Maitland said, "I'm not a murderer."

Frank Chang said, "Earlier, you called me an assassin. A killer. I don't take offense at the term. This evening, you killed two men. And I suspect they weren't the first men you've killed."

"This evening was different."

"Yes," Frank said. "They had abducted your friend. Perhaps someone you think of as family. Yes?"

". . . yes."

"You acted to protect family. Preston Wong, in his way, will do the same thing."

Maitland shook his head. He said, "You're asking me to get mixed up in some sort of gang war."

"You've already mixed yourself up in it. I'm not a priest, Maitland. I have no interest in persuading you that it's moral or

252

virtuous to kill Preston Wong or his men. I'm only telling you what you're dealing with."

"You want me to help you get your money from them so you can 'save face.' Or take vengeance. I'm not interested in doing that."

"Okay," Frank said. "I'll let you think about it for a while. But remember, you may need me too."

He kept the gun pointed at Maitland as he got to his feet. With his other hand he took out a little spiral notebook and threw it on the coffee table. He threw a pen down after it.

Then he said, "Write down your cell number, and I'll call you."

Maitland did so and Frank Chang picked up the pad and paper.

He was at the door when Maitland stopped him.

"Hey," Maitland said.

Frank said, "What?"

"Where are my guns?"

"They're under the kitchen sink," Frank said. "Leave them there for a few minutes." He walked out, closing the door after him.

Maitland got off the couch and looked at the closed door.

The man could be standing right behind it, his Browning pointing at it. He could have walked down to the next floor on the staircase, stopping halfway with his body shielded behind the banister, ready to shoot at someone coming for him. He could be gone. Out of the building.

Maitland sighed. He walked over to the kitchen sink and opened the cabinet beneath it. Next to the dishwashing liquid and the box of Clorox was his "mare's leg" shotgun, his .38, and his .45. Later, when he went to his desk to check his ammunition, he found that a box of his .45 rounds was missing.

Well, Maitland thought, that was the only thing he took.

TWENTY-SEVEN

Maitland thought, load one of the guns and run down the stairs. Maybe the guy's standing at the corner waiting for the bus. Point the gun at him, take away his weapon, and say, "Now, let's talk."

Do that. And then what?

What would the man say that was any different? What would he add? He had had the drop on Maitland cold. He could have plugged him in his own apartment and that would have been that. He could have, but he didn't.

Did that mean he had been telling the truth?

Had he been with the one called Hsu-shen, he would have done that. He would have killed Maitland and then left. Gone back to his buddies and said, "You can't believe how easy it was." You need to get an alarm, Maitland thought. The guns weren't much of a protection when someone got

255

home before you did and hid them. Someone who would think to do that. A professional.

The guy hadn't said his name. He'd admitted that he was the one that killed Raymond Liu. He more or less admitted that he had killed the men at Ravinia's. Fucking Chinese triad assassin sitting in his living room, holding a gun while he talked Chinese philosophy.

Telling him, they're going to kill your woman. They're going to kill your friend. Telling him that it didn't matter that she was innocent. Ending her life. Ending the life of a woman who had never done anything to harm anyone. Ending the life of someone he cared about. Telling Maitland that he could pat himself on the back for saving her today. But that these were the sort of guys that would probably come back tomorrow. And the day after that, and the day after that until they got it done.

Telling him that these guys were working for Preston Wong.

Preston Wong. Who the fuck was he?

Some guy who was in the papers a lot. Well, maybe not a lot. But once in a while in the society pages. Fundraisers, balls . . . wearing a nice suit and standing with his attractive wife with Dr. and Mrs. Somebody

Else. Pretty people. The sort Bianca said made good clients because they had money and were willing to spend it on high-dollar antiques.

A Chinese American. From San Francisco, not the Chinese underworld. A "white" bread–type of fellow.

Right?

Maitland remembered something of Chinese gangs from his days working narcotics. He remembered being at one of those wrong places at the wrong time when a group of young blacks squared off against a group of young Chinese. The Chinese seemed to look younger than they were. Slight, quiet, but one of the blacks said, "Fucking Chink" and that was when the swinging started and the Chinese just wiped up the floor with them. Kicks and fast punches and Maitland thought that sort of thing only happened in the movies. But the Chinese won, and decisively.

Maitland had once worked patrol with an older cop who was something of a war history buff. The guy's name had been Bowen and during long, tedious shifts he liked to go on about the personality differences between MacArthur and Patton and Eisenhower and the bland Omar Bradley. Bowen said that Truman was wrong to relieve Mac-

Arthur of command and that the truth was the man had an understanding of Asia that Truman never did. Bowen said that, of course, race was an issue in the Second World War. That both the Japanese and the Americans thought the other was an inferior race. Until Pearl Harbor, most Americans, the brilliant MacArthur included, could not comprehend that these squat little yellow men would be able to outsmart them or surprise them, let alone overrun them. But Bowen also stressed that the Japanese thought the Americans were just a bunch of overfed, dipshit round-eyes. Both underestimated the other.

Maitland thought, Preston Wong's not Japanese. He's Chinese.

But Maitland was thinking about Bowen's words now. For Maitland, it was hard to comprehend that this soft-looking, wealthy Chinese American could be the criminal kingpin the assassin made him out to be. It didn't make sense. Wong looked like a lawyer or a businessman.

Maitland remembered the party he had given. Only a few days ago. Bianca had given him an invitation. Maitland remembered putting it in his desk drawer.

It was still there. The time and address written on it.

Maitland got the .45 and the .38 and walked down the back stairs to the garage. He took the '75 Pontiac, leaving the BMW in the garage.

On the first pass by Wong's mansion, Maitland saw two guards. He did not risk a second pass. He parked the car four blocks away and walked back. He saw two more guards near the house then. Maitland figured there would be more inside. Preston Wong was well protected.

Maitland walked back to the Pontiac.

Driving back north, he wondered just what the assassin had in mind. Would he have Maitland go in through the front door, take shots from the various bodyguards while he went through the back and squared it with Wong? Would he use Maitland as a decoy? Did it matter to the assassin if Maitland lived or died? If Bianca lived or died?

The assassin was suggesting that Maitland throw in with him. Using Bianca as bait. Maitland would protect his friend, the assassin would get his money, save face. Not a bad idea, if the assassin was being truthful. And then the assassin would leave town and Maitland would be stuck with an indictment for murder. His defense being that a Chinese ghost told him that triads don't buy the notion of being Good Samaritans.

They used to say that this was one of the risks of being undercover in narcotics. You spend so much time acting like the enemy, thinking like the enemy, that you risk becoming the enemy yourself. Cops becoming part of the drug cartel themselves. Wong had been a policeman. But the assassin said he had not merely taken payoffs. He was part of the triad almost from the beginning.

Maitland had been accused of going native himself. Had been accused of taking money from a dealer and then killing the dealer to cover it up. He was innocent and he was cleared. But he knew that there were still people at Chicago PD who thought he was guilty.

He had never been so self-pitying to think that he wished he had been crooked. That sort of thinking was for losers. When he had been undercover, he had never felt tempted. He had never feared going native. He had killed a dealer in self-defense and he had regretted having to do it. On some level, he had grown to like the guy.

Still, just because he had kept clean, it didn't mean that all cops would have done the same. If anything, his experience in Kansas had taught him that cops could be easily corrupted. Particularly if there was drug money involved. It was probably dumb to assume that Wong had been "turned." He had probably known his intentions all along.

Maitland had his gun drawn when he got back to his apartment. He checked every bit of it before he got into bed to go to sleep.

Twenty-Eight

First thing the next morning, he called Bianca at her home. The phone was ringing and he wondered what he would say if Max answered it. He told himself that Max would have slept it off by now.

No matter, though. It was Bianca who answered the phone.

"Hey," Maitland said. "Is everything all right?"

"Yes. Max left for work."

Maitland paused, wondering what was and what was not his business. He said, "He went to work?"

"Yes. He's . . . he always makes it to work."

"Well, I'm sure he's been stressed over this," Maitland said, trying to step around it.

But Bianca said, "No. He's done this before. Look, I don't want to burden you with it."

"It's all right. Listen," he said, "I don't

think you should go in today."

"Why? Are you worried?"

"Yeah, kind of. Do you mind if I come over?"

"What for?"

"I just want to talk to you."

"You want to talk me into leaving, don't you?"

"Just for a while."

Bianca said, "You're welcome to try."

He was driving against traffic coming into the city, but it still took him three quarters of an hour to get to her house. She let him in and asked him if he wanted some coffee. He sat at her kitchen table while she made it. A simple thing, but it was new to him. He had never sat at her table in her home in the morning. Her serving him . . . it was like they were married. Domestic. Too domestic.

Bianca sat across from him. She had her cappuccino and a small piece of coffee cake, which she ate with a fork. She said, "I'm sorry about last night."

Maitland said, "There's nothing to be sorry for."

"He's my husband. And this is our home."

"Don't worry about it."

"He does that sometimes."

"Drinks?"

"Yes."

"Like I said before, it's a stressful time."

"For him, it's always stressful." She paused. "I guess I'm betraying him, talking about his problem with you."

Maitland said, "It's none of my business."

She had always been so private. She never discussed her marriage. And it was news to Maitland that Max was a boozer. He felt embarrassed for her. She had always conveyed such strength and poise. A shield of sorts.

She was looking at her coffee cake now. She said, "He's not a bad man, Evan."

"I know."

Bianca said, "He's just a little weak, sometimes. The drinking . . . I know it's not a character defect, but sometimes . . ."

Sometimes it's hard to forget that, Maitland thought. But he didn't say it. Her husband was sober now and he had left her alone in the house.

Maitland said, "I didn't know."

And she said, "How would you?"

"I don't know."

"Well, I'm not leaving him, if that's what you're thinking."

"I wasn't saying you should," Maitland said. "That's not why I came here. What I

264

mean is, I want you to leave this house for a day or two. Until this thing calms down."

"This thing?" she said. "Do you know what it is?"

"I'm working on it," Maitland said.

She looked at him and smiled. Her first one of the day. Sometimes she smiled at him in a way that mocked him. *Go to Cleveland, shoot somebody.* But there was no teasing now.

"Bianca."

"Yes?"

"Don't freak out or anything, but a man came to my apartment last night. A Chinese guy. Tall and with a dark suit. His eyes were a sort of gray."

She was looking back at him, her jaw dropping slightly.

Maitland said, "He sort of admitted to me that he was the guy that killed Raymond Liu."

"You mean the one that let me go?"

"Yes."

"Oh. Oh my God. He came to your home? . . . How?"

"He must have seen me on the news. I don't know. He found me, though. I don't think he's after you. He says there's . . . some sort of war going on between two Chinese gangs. Mafias. And that you've been caught in between."

"Have you told the police?"

"No."

After a moment, Bianca said, "Have you told Julie?"

"No."

She was looking at him now, waiting for him to elaborate on that one. He didn't, though. She said, "Why not?"

He trusted Julie with his life. But things were strange between them now. He said, "I don't know, exactly. She's a good friend and she's loyal to me. But . . . it's just not a good idea to tell her."

"But she's your girlfriend. Your lover."

Maitland said, "I'm not so sure that's true anymore."

"I'm sorry, Evan."

"Well, I'm sorry too. The long and the short of it is, her relationship with me was compromising her career. Besides, it's . . . well, it's complicated."

"Because of me?"

"Yeah. Partly that. It's other things too."

Bianca said, "It's not my business, Evan, but I want to ask, was it your idea?"

"Was what my idea?"

"Was it your idea to end it?"

Maitland shrugged. "Ah, what difference does it make? The circumstances were clos-

266

ing in on us. She can rise in the police department or she can stay with me. But she can't do both."

"Did you ask her what it is she wanted?"

"No."

Bianca said, "Maybe you should've."

"Ask her what? To marry me?"

"What?" Bianca laughed. "No. That's not what I meant."

"Is that idea so funny?"

"No," she said. "Well, yes. Sort of. God, you confuse things sometimes."

"You're the one confusing things. What did you mean?"

"I didn't mean you should have asked her to marry you. That would have been a terrible idea."

"It would have?"

"Yes. Gosh, you're so dense sometimes."

"She might have married me."

"Yeah, if she was insane."

"Hey."

"I'm sorry, but really, Evan. You never wanted to marry her."

"How are you so sure of that?"

"Well, I'm not completely blind. You've known her for almost two years now and . . . I mean, come on."

"She's a great lady."

"Of course she is. And she deserves a good

267

man. But you're not the man."

"Why not?"

"You're just not."

"You were the one that encouraged me to pursue her. Way back when."

"Sure, I did. I didn't mean for you to marry her. Or live with her."

"What was wrong with that?"

"Look, it's not my place."

"Well, we're in it now. You just as well give me it all."

"Evan." She paused. "She saved your life, right?"

"Right."

"There's the problem. You owe her because of that. That's gratitude and affection, but it's not the basis for a long-term commitment. You had to know that."

"There was more than that. We were drawn to each other. Certainly attracted to each other. Shit. I feel bad."

"For what?"

"I don't know. Wasting her time, I guess."

"Oh," Bianca said, "don't flatter yourself. From what you told me, she was going to divorce that asshole whether or not you were in the picture. You Americans, you think too much in terms of marriage and whether or not you're 'wasting time.' She had a good time with you and you had a good time with her. What is it you think you took from her? Time?"

"Well, maybe . . ."

"No. If she wanted to marry someone else, she would have sought that out. Just so long as you didn't mislead her. You didn't, did you?"

"I don't think I did."

"Good. Then get over yourself."

Maitland said, "Uh, yeah, I'll try." He had not been expecting this European form of cheering up.

Bianca picked up her plate and put it in the sink. From there, she said, "Evan."

"Yeah?"

"I am frightened."

"Don't be," he said. "I'll get it worked out."

She remained at the sink and he remained seated at the table. It occurred to Maitland then that he had never seen her cry. They had had a fight once, when a couple of men had tried to kill him as he came out of the store. She hadn't been there, but he had inadvertently brought violence near her world. She had really let him have it and was as upset as he had ever seen her. But she hadn't cried. If she did so now, he would go to her and take her in his arms. He would not be able to stop himself.

She didn't cry, though.

And Maitland said, "Charlie has a place at Lake Geneva. He's told me we can use it."

"For a romantic weekend?"

"I wouldn't be staying with you. I just want you to stay there for a day or two."

"I was kidding, Evan."

"Max could stay with you."

"I know. I was kidding."

Maitland said, "Just for a day or two. While I work on things."

Bianca said, "I can't hide forever, you know. I won't do that."

"I'm not asking you to," Maitland said. "But for now, will you do this for me?"

Bianca said, "Okay, Evan."

He drove her to a cottage near the Wisconsin lake. She had protested this at first, saying that without her own car there would be no way for her to even drive to the store if she needed to. She said she didn't mind hiding out for a couple of days, but she certainly wasn't going to become a prisoner. Maitland said he understood her concern, but there was a convenience store within walking distance of the cottage and her car could probably indentify her. She said, "You mean they'll find me here?" And Maitland said not to talk like that because it was silly and would she for once not fucking argue with him.

So they drove to Wisconsin in angry silence, Bianca spending almost the entire trip looking out her window. Partly Maitland was relieved by this because if she was quiet maybe she wouldn't take the trouble to ask him specifically what he was going to do. He wasn't sure himself.

He wanted to call his old friend at DEA, Jay Jackson, and see what they had found out about the Ravinia murders. But before he picked up his phone to do it, he realized that odds were good he knew more about it than Jay did. The man who was at his apartment last night had been at Ravinia's too, talking around things but more or less admitting that he had been responsible for what happened there.

Maitland told himself, the man said he hadn't killed the DEA agent. He just said he'd been there when it happened.

So. Call Jay Jackson and tell him that.

And Jay Jackson would say, why didn't you call the police right away?

And Maitland could say, well, he wasn't sure he believed the guy.

Which would be a lie. He did believe the guy. And now that he had spoken to Bianca

271

about it, it was confirmed that it was the same guy who had let her go. The guy who had been at Raymond Liu's and the guy who had been at Ravinia's. And Maitland's first order of business had been to get Bianca to safety.

And Jay Jackson might say, seems like you got your priorities mixed up.

Not so much.

Driving back to Chicago, Maitland thought, *But I'm not a cop anymore.*

What did he owe them? They had done little more than give him grief the last few days. And hadn't they betrayed him when he was on the force? He remembered Sam Stillman giving him roughly the same lecture his union lawyer had given him years earlier. The basic premise being that cops and even ex-cops could be fools when it came to not knowing when to assert the Fifth and keeping their fucking mouths shut. Sam Stillman said, "You guys are all alike. They say to you, 'Just tell us what happened and we'll get it all straightened out.' Using the same tricks you used when you were on the force. *And you still fall for it.* They're not seeking the truth. They only want to incriminate you."

But Jay Jackson was a good guy. And Julie Ciskowski was nothing if not decent. They were the sort that wanted to help, not harass good people into trouble with the law. Maitland thought, you could call Jay and tell him . . . part of it.

But part truths were lies and there was no getting around that. Martha Stewart went to jail not for insider trading, but for lying to federal investigators and, more specifically, trying to lead them off the trail. She could have asserted the Fifth Amendment and refused to answer any questions and she probably would have been fine. Not because she was clean, but because they would probably not have had enough evidence on the initial charge to file a case against her. But she tried to outsmart them and it got her hammered.

He could call Jay and tell him part of it, but then he'd be lying to Jay, lying to a friend to protect another friend and maybe that was okay, but not if it led to a jail sentence.

He could call Julie and tell her about it. Tell her about the conversation he had with the assassin in his apartment. The apartment she had slept at the night before.

Oh . . . maybe not. He had already done enough to her.

Call Jay and tell him everything. Leave nothing out.

It would mean, at a minimum, five to six hours in interrogation. Being asked the same questions from different investigators from DEA, FBI, state and city police. People suspecting him for not saying something earlier. And sooner or later one of them would bring up the past, his alleged graft taking from drug dealers and that shady business with the Jamaicans. And if he was lucky, maybe it would end with them saying, watch your step next time, buddy. But he was picturing a jail cell in county, Sam Stillman coming to see him, shaking his head and saying, "I *told* you."

Maitland got back to Chicago and stopped at a diner for lunch. He ordered a ham sandwich and chips and when the waitress left him alone, he took a discarded newspaper off the next table. The local section told him that Preston Wong and his wife were hosting a fundraiser for Congressman Tasset this coming Saturday.

Twenty-Nine

There were six cabs lined up in the front drive of the Sheraton Chicago Hotel. Some yellow, some painted red and white. They would move up in line as the guests would walk out and take one and the doorman would signal the next cab to pull ahead. It was an easy thirty-dollar fare to the airport and they would pick up another one there.

Maitland walked out of the hotel and the doorman gestured him toward the front cab.

"No, thank you," Maitland said and walked back along the line. The doorman said, "Sir?" But Maitland kept walking, slowed, and then got into the fifth cab.

Closed the door himself.

"O'Hare," Maitland said.

The cabby didn't say anything, put the gear in drive, and pulled out past the other cabs. Made the turnaround and then made the left turn onto Water Street.

They were crossing over the Chicago River when Maitland said, "You been doing all right, Ricky?"

It was then that Richard Cavazos looked into the rearview mirror. Frowned and said, "Man, what the fuck you want?"

Maitland said, "I just want to talk to you, that's all."

"I haven't done nothing."

Maitland leaned forward and put two hundred-dollar bills through the plastic window. He said, "Just take it, okay?"

Cavazos reached over his right shoulder to snatch the bills. He was a practiced cabby by now, but Maitland was ready and he held onto them.

Maitland said, "You gotta earn it, Ricky."

Three years ago, Ricky Cavazos had jumped bail after being arrested for possession with intent to distribute. Maitland found him in a third-floor walk-up in Milwaukee. Cavazos had surrendered peacefully, saying he'd had enough of Milwaukee anyway. Not a fighter by nature, but no pushover either. The prosecutors said he could have a six-month suspended sentence if he would tell them the name of his suppliers and Ricky Cavazos told them to go fuck themselves, he wasn't going to die for them. They gave him a two-year state sentence, and he went in for fourteen months before he got parole.

Maitland brought him back and collected his fee, but stayed out of it beyond that. Still, he knew as well as the cops that Cavazos had been working for Perfidio Chavez, the leader of what the feds called the Mexican Mafia because they hadn't come up with a better name.

Now Ricky said, "Earn it? How — floatin' in the river? I'm making an honest living."

"Me too," Maitland said. "And I ain't asking you to roll on anyone."

"What do you want, then?"

"Take me to Perfidio."

"Who's that?"

Maitland laughed. You had to hand it to the guy, saying it with a straight face. "Come on," Maitland said. "I just want to talk to him."

"You trying to catch someone else now?"

"No. I'm coming in good faith."

"You lie to me, man, that's one thing. You lie to Perfidio, that's bad. You know what I'm saying?"

"I know. Look, I'm not on the clock now."

"You carrying?"

"No," he lied.

" 'Cause they're going to ask me that."

"Like I told you," Maitland said. He

released the bills. "I'm coming in good faith."

Cavazos stopped the cab at a phone booth off Rush Street. He was talking for about ten minutes while Maitland sat in the cab, the meter running the whole time. Cavazos came back and said, "Okay. He might talk to you."

"Might?"

"I'll take you there, and then you're on your own."

Minutes later, the cab came out of the underpass from Michigan Avenue and onto North Lake Shore Drive. Sun filled up the interior and then the lake was on their right. People on Oak Street Beach sitting in the sand because the water was too rough and cold, rollerbladers and bicycles moving up and down the path. There were others doing the same thing all the way up to the North Avenue beach, the vast blue lake opening up.

Cavazos got off on the Fullerton Avenue exit. He made a lot of stops and starts, cars moving in front of him over speed bumps as they got close to Diversey Harbor. Big yachts and white sailboats with their masts sticking up like stripped trees and it was a beautiful Chicago summer day, but Maitland was feeling uneasy about it.

And then Cavazos stopped the cab and said, "Okay. You want to go down pier seventeen, slip number thirty."

Maitland paid the fare and got out. He walked out to the piers and checked his pocket for his .45. It was still there. About a six-hundred-dollar gun. If they found it on him, they might get their feelings hurt and go to work on him. If they took no offense, they'd simply throw it overboard and he'd have to buy another one. He put it between a couple of white storage boxes and scooted the boxes together to hide it. Then he walked down to pier seventeen.

He saw the crew as he approached the slip and within a second saw that they saw him too. Two hard-looking Mexicans on the boat, one of them not wearing a shirt as he set a crate down. The other one wearing a jacket in the summer and he straightened up when he saw Maitland walking up to the boat. It was this one who spoke first.

"You the bounty hunter?"

"Not today," Maitland said.

The Mexican patted a place beneath his jacket, signaling that he had a gun there. Maitland nodded. The Mexican gestured for Maitland to raise his hands above his head. Maitland did and then the younger one stepped up and patted him down. He didn't find any weapons, so he turned around and so gestured to the one in the boat.

The Mexican said, "Step aboard."

Maitland did.

The Mexican said, "Take off your jacket."

Maitland took off his jacket and handed it to the younger one. The younger one handed it to the older Mexican. The Mexican took Maitland's cell phone out of the jacket pocket and threw it into the water. Then he said, "Take off your shirt too."

Maitland took off his shirt and handed it to the younger one. He turned around to show them he wasn't wearing a wire. He had forgotten about the phone. Those could be used as recording devices too, and often were by informants.

"Okay," the Mexican said. He gestured to Maitland's clothes, saying he could put them back on. He pointed to the back bench of the yacht and said, "You sit there."

That was all he said and then the younger one was casting off lines. Maitland looked up to see another crew member at the wheel and then the engines turned and caught and then were burbling with life, churning the water beneath them.

Maitland thought, *fuck*.

The Mexican with the jacket sat across from him and folded his legs. And then the boat was moving slowly up the harbor to the inlet and then under Lake Shore Drive. Maitland thought about asking if Perfidio was even on board, but then the inlet was behind them and the engines went full throttle as they went out into the great lake and he knew he wasn't going to be talking to anyone until they were miles away from shore. And if they got out there and threw him over, he would never be found.

THIRTY

From time to time, he would glance back at the shore, watching it shrink in size. Soon, people could no longer be discerned. Then Lake Shore traffic faded out. Then they were miles out and the Chicago skyline was a distant mountain range.

The engines throttled back and then cut. Waves sloshed against the prow of the boat and the foam of the wake settled back into the water.

"It gets hot out here when the boat is sitting, huh?"

It was Perfidio Chavez. He had come up the stairs of the cabin to stand on the back deck. He wore white pants and a yellow shirt, flapping open in the wind. Unlike his men, he was not clean-shaven. He had one of those bad early seventies' beards, like George Harrison's at his *Bangladesh* concert.

Maitland said, "Yeah, pretty hot. I guess

you're going to suggest I take a swim?"

Perfidio Chavez laughed. He said, "You think you can make it back?"

"I'll take a few breaks, rest on my back."

"Yeah, tell yourself you're just going to close your eyes for a few moments to take a nap. That's when you sink. I tell myself, this fuckin' guy is either stupid or he's got cojones like Camacho."

"Camacho got beat."

"Yeah?" Perfidio Chavez smiled. "By who?"

"De la Hoya. I saw it."

"Man, he's too fucking old to fight De la Hoya. He says he's going to retire. You believe that?"

"I haven't given it any thought."

"You do any boxing yourself?"

"No."

Perfidio Chavez moved to the back of the boat and looked out over the water. He said, "You know, there is a third possibility."

Maitland said, "What's that?"

"That you're in the business, yourself."

Maitland said, "Dealing?"

"Yes."

"Why would you think that?"

Perfidio Chavez said, "I knew a guy years ago, he used to hang around Hector's gym, watch the fights. His name was Leo and he was the biggest fucking crook in the state. You know what his cover was?"

"Yeah," Maitland said. "He was a bail bondsman."

Perfidio nodded at the water.

Maitland said, "That's not my game."

Perfidio Chavez turned to look at him. "No?" he said. "I heard about you."

"What did you hear?"

"That you put down Ronnie Ellis."

"That's right." Maitland wasn't going to elaborate on that. He knew enough to know that these two men had not been friends. He looked back at Perfidio, his expression calm and passive.

Perfidio said, "Aren't you going to tell me he had it coming?"

"No."

The man smiled again. "Well, he did. What do you want with me, bond man?"

"Preston Wong. What do you know about him?"

"Preston — ?"

"Wong. The leader of the Wu-Chai Triad."

". . . who?"

"Look, if you don't want to tell me, just say so. But don't fucking act like you don't know."

The Mexican with the gun in his waistband was staring at him now. Waiting, just waiting, for Perfidio to give him a sign.

Perfidio looked at his man briefly, but then made a gesture that said, not now. He said, "You say you not a cop?"

"Yes."

"And you're not in the trade?"

"No."

"Then why do you want to know?"

Maitland said, "That's private."

Perfidio said, "We got nothing but privacy out here, man."

Maitland said nothing.

Perfidio said, "You know, some men try to talk tough to hide their fear. You scared, Maitland?"

Maitland smiled. "Sure," he said. "Tell me what you want to know."

"There's a rumor that Wong is trying to take over the heroin market in Chicago. Is that true?"

Perfidio Chavez sat in a chair near Maitland. In so doing, he put himself between his bodyguard and Maitland. An intended gesture.

Perfidio said, "Yes, it's true. The word is, he had a couple of people killed who were working for another triad. The Red Lantern. You heard of them?"

"Yes."

"They killed the Red Lantern's head chef.

They can't replace him. Now with the *hermanos* or the Colombians, you do that and you got a full-scale fucking war. But the Chinese, they don't work like that. They do that and *afterward,* they sit down and negotiate. It's fucked up, man."

"Is Wong really in charge, or is he just sort of a respectable front?"

"No, man, he's in charge. Make no mistake about that."

"You believe he ordered those hits?"

"Of course. Man, he has an edge. The Anglos, they see us, and they run away. But they'll accept someone like him. 'Cause he looks like them. Well, not like them. But they think they know him, see?"

"Yeah."

Perfidio said, "Is he after you? 'Cause if he is, you may as well leave the fucking state. They don't give up."

Maitland said, "Where is the farm?"

"The farm. You mean, where do they refine their heroin? Man, how the fuck should I know? And if I did know, I wouldn't tell you. I don't want a fight with them."

Maitland wasn't going to argue that point. He was hoping to get a nonconfirmation from this man. Hoping to hear that Preston Wong was harmless. Hoping to hear that he *was* merely a front man. It would have been

286

better that way. Maybe then he could have told himself that Bianca was safe. That he was overreacting.

Maitland said, "They killed their opponent's chemist, right?"

"Yeah."

"That must mean they have their own."

"Yeah. They got one. From San Francisco, I think."

"You know where he's at?"

Perfidio smiled again. "Man," he said, "what are you going to get yourself into?"

"Do you know who he is?"

Perfidio Chavez sighed. He slapped his hands lightly on his knees, giving up. He said, "It's not a he."

THIRTY-ONE

He picked her up coming out of her apartment in the Bucktown section. He walked about a block behind her, as they went past the dog park. He hoped she wouldn't hail a cab because his car wasn't parked very close and he would have to hail another cab to keep a tail on her.

But a block later, he saw her turn to the staircase that led to the Blue Line elevated train. He followed her up the stairs and paid for a ticket. After he went through the turnstiles, he bought a newspaper and put his external focus on that as he kept an eye on her. She boarded the train and Maitland folded his newspaper and did the same.

The train moved southeast, downtown, and Maitland remained on his feet, one hand gripping the pole as he got a better look at her.

She was a bit younger than he thought she'd be. Maybe thirty. An attractive young lady with a remote, cool air about her. Her name was Lee Qin and she had a degree in chemistry from San Jose State University. Her hair was shoulder-length and she wore a short black skirt with a black cotton shirt. She looked like she could be a graduate student.

Maitland wondered if she was. Perfidio having fun with him.

She did what attractive city girls usually do on trains. Avoided eye contact, looked out the window, gave the oglers no encouragement. And the more Maitland took her in, the more trouble he had with it. She simply didn't look like a criminal. He anticipated following her to a club on Rush Street, watching her order margaritas with her friends and talk about what bands they liked. Time wasted.

But then she got off the train at the Clark terminal and switched over to the Red Line south. Maitland stayed with her, stalking, but keeping out of sight and if she busted him and called a cop, he'd shrug his shoulders and say he didn't even know this girl. But nothing like that happened and he felt better when she got off her seat as they approached the Cermak-Chinatown exit.

Could mean nothing, he thought. Could mean she's got family there.

He walked behind through Chinatown and here it got a little tricky. The sidewalks were crowded with vendors and buyers and the sun was coming down as well. It was not easy to keep her in sight, young Asian woman wearing black, but she wasn't the only one. And if he got too close, she might turn around and see that he was the same one she had noticed on the train.

He still had her in his sights though when she made an arc and went into a small grocery shop.

Maitland slowed his walk, but kept going. He stopped in front of the shop and faced the street. There was no window for him to look through. There was only a wall with a small decorative tile on it. A red pelican holding a frog's leg in its mouth, the frog dangling upside down, unable to escape.

Maitland thought, if he walked in, she would see him. There would be no hiding then.

A truck rolled by and before it had passed, he had gone in.

The shop was small and self-contained, no more than half the size of a suburban convenience store. Shelves of Chinese goods in orange and blue boxes, things that had been imported from Hong Kong and the

Mainland and could not ordinarily be purchased in an American supermarket. In the center of the store, there was fresh fish lying in a crate of ice.

The only people there were two men behind the cashier's counter. One of them was slight and around forty years of age and he wore a white apron. He stood in front of the cash register. A second man, bigger and younger, stood behind him, his hands at his side.

Lee Qin acknowledged them when she came in. The cashier nodded back and Lee Qin proceeded to the back. She got to a steel door at the back door and the cashier pressed a switch under the counter. The steel door opened and Lee Qin disappeared behind it.

Lee Qin went down a narrow passageway and turned right into a small room. In the room, there were two television screens on the wall. Both of them displayed grainy black and white images. One was of the front of the store. The second one revealed the inside of the store. This was the security room.

Hsu-shen was there with two of his men.

Lee Qin said, "Well?"

Hsu-shen said, "He needs to meet with you."

"Okay," she said.

Hsu-shen said, "Go with Chen. He will escort you."

Lee Qin walked out and Chen followed her. They continued down the narrow hall. Opened another door at the end of it and walked down a flight of steps into a small garage. A Ford cargo van was parked there. Chen and Lee Qin got in the back doors. Another man started the van. The garage door opened and they drove out the back, the door coming down after them.

Back in the security room, Hsu-shen and the second man looked at the video screens. The routine always required that Lee Qin come through this place or another place like it. Wong owned all of them. It took a lot of time when Wong wanted to meet with Lee Qin or wanted her transported to a lab, but it was a necessary precaution. Security was essential.

Hsu-shen leaned forward, seeing something on the screen that caught his attention.

A white man, through the front door, now looking up and down the aisles.

Hsu-shen said, "I don't believe it."

THIRTY-TWO

The store was small. Four aisles with shelves about seven feet high. Maitland walked the width and didn't see the girl. He looked out at the open area where the fish sat across from the boxed fruit. She wasn't there either.

Strange.

He looked back to the front door. Then at the two men behind the counter, the second one looking back at him with an unpleasant expression. He was unwelcome here.

Where had the girl gone?

Maitland walked down the second aisle. He came to the end and saw a corridor leading to a heavy closed door. And then he heard it before he saw it. The door coming unlocked and his heart skipped a beat, his body sensing it before his mind, and then the door was opening and a man was coming out of it with a stubby machine gun, bringing it up —

Maitland moved to his left, out of the range of the man with the machine gun, but the guy let out a burst anyway, thacking rounds into the dried noodles and bottles of cooking wine. Maitland moved around the fourth aisle, the one against the wall. He crouched, his thoughts now on the front door and running to it, but he looked up at the circular mirror hanging from the ceiling corner and as he did, he heard a man call out commands in Chinese and after that, the menacing-looking one who had been behind the counter went to the front door and locked the bolt.

Christ, Maitland thought. They were trapping him.

The two guys from the counter brought weapons out themselves. The younger one now handing a semiautomatic to the cashier. And then he was getting a Remington shotgun, pumping a round into the chamber, making that awful *shick-shick* sound. They came out from the counter, coming closer, and then the same Chinese voice called out another command and they stopped.

Silence.

Maitland was in a sitting position now, his back against the shelf. He had his Glock .45 out, waiting for the first man to come around the corner.

More silence.

And then a voice, speaking firmly in English.

"Mr. Maitland, what are you doing here?"

Maitland said, "Who's asking?"

"We have never met," Hsu-shen said. "Not formally. You tried to shoot me."

Maitland said, "Was that you?"

"Yeah. That was me."

Maitland said, "I'm sorry I missed."

Hsu-shen smiled. He said, "I should have killed you before we took the woman. But I thought you were nobody."

"I am nobody."

"You had surprise on your side that day. Not today, though." Hsu-shen said, "Why don't you tell us where the woman is? Maybe then, we'll let you live."

"I'd like that," Maitland said. "But I don't know where she is."

Hsu-shen said, "You're a fool. You've walked right into this. You can get out, though, if you're willing to be reasonable. Tell us where she is."

Maitland looked up at the mirror. The young one with the shotgun was stepping closer to the corner.

Hsu-shen said, "We know she's been hidden. We know you're protecting her."

The shotgun man took another step.

"But she's not yours to protect, is she?" Hsu-shen said. "She doesn't belong to you."

The man with the shotgun placed his foot around the corner of the aisle. It stayed there. Maitland shook his head and sighed before he lifted his .45 and fired.

The shot echoed in the small store, the man dropped the shotgun as the bullet shattered the arch of his foot. He hopped back to the counter, howling in pain. Careless.

Maitland looked in the mirror. The cashier was still there, holding his pistol on the corner for when Maitland came out.

And Maitland was thinking, he could put a foot on one of the shelves and step up so that he could see over it and maybe shoot the cashier and when the cashier went down, he could rush for the front door.

But the front door was bolted shut. Even if it required no key to unlock, he would be at the door, delayed, before he could get it open. The door was locked and he could get it open if he had time, but they would shoot him before he could. Guy with a machine gun, the leader who was probably armed too, and the guy with the shotgun, who was probably wondering if he'd ever feel his toes again.

But he quit thinking about it when the

296

guy with the machine gun came around the corner of the other side of the aisle raising his machine gun and firing anywhere down the aisle, but not hitting and Maitland fired two shots back and the guy flicked back behind the shelf and then Maitland was up and running for the other end and he got there and dove to the ground, sliding as the cashier fired at him and Maitland fired back, from the floor, and caught the cashier with a shot to the chest. The cashier went down and Maitland turned and looked down the next aisle, looking for the guy with the machine gun, not seeing him and then looking for him in the corner mirror and that was when he felt the numbing thud of pain in his wrist and watched as his gun fell out of his hand and clattered to the floor.

He turned to see Hsu-shen, a short, compact man, not armed apparently, and then one of his arms became a blur as it shot out to Maitland's face.

Maitland's eyes were closed when he hit the ground, but he had just enough consciousness left in him to feel his head bounce off the ground. That was all he remembered.

THIRTY-THREE

Julie was saying, "I told you." Looking at him from across a table, her expression disappointed and angry. And at first, he thought he was alone. But the table widened and now Sam Stillman was there as well, sitting on Maitland's side of the table, saying "Let him alone." Maitland wanting to say something to her, wondering why he had brought Sam along. He didn't need Sam to protect himself against Julie, she wasn't after him for anything. He wanted to tell Sam that he hadn't meant for him to be here. That if he'd called him, it had been a mistake. It was just Julie. She was angry at him, but it was not in an official capacity. They shouldn't be hiding things from her. He shouldn't be bringing lawyers to the table when he met with her. Maybe that's why she was angry with him now. Brings a fucking lawyer . . .

A pain in his shin.

Jesus, Sam.

Another kick. This one harder.

He opened his eyes.

"Wake up," a voice said.

And now Maitland was conscious of another pain. His head throbbing.

Hsu-shen kicked him again.

"Wake up. You can wake up now."

Maitland lifted his head.

He was in a wooden chair. His arms were tied behind his back. There were half a dozen men in the room with him.

Maitland looked around. There were windows and it was dark out. He could see trees and not much else. He knew he was on the second floor of a house. But he couldn't see any other houses in the distance. They were someplace rural. A farm perhaps.

Most of the men in the room were armed. Men leaning against the wall, some of them with guns tucked into their belts, one of them holding a shotgun by the stock. The two men in front of him did not seem to be armed. One of them was the one that had hit him. The other was dressed in a full suit, looking like he had someplace better to be.

Maitland said, "Mister Wong."

Preston Wong looked at him and shook his head. It was a cop's gesture that Maitland was familiar with. He'd used it himself in his time. The policeman's way of telling the naughty boy he'd been caught. A way of putting him in his place.

"Evan," Wong said.

That was a cop thing too. Using a subject's first name to belittle him. A man addressing a wayward child.

Preston Wong said, "You've been a nuisance."

"Have I? I don't mean to be."

"Three of my men killed," Wong said. "And another one with part of his foot shot off. Their friends would like to say something to you."

"I'm sure they would."

"In time, Evan. In time. Tell me, how did you know about the girl?"

"Which girl?"

"Lee Qin."

"I didn't know anything about her."

Wong sighed. He made a gesture to Hsu-shen and Hsu-shen slapped Maitland across the face.

Wong said, "You were following her."

Maitland said, "Well, she's quite a looker."

Wong said, "Were you trying to find me? Yes? Well, here I am. What did you want to talk about?"

Maitland said, "I'm not sure. I was hoping maybe I could talk some sense into you."

Wong smiled. "Sense? What is it you can tell me?"

"I was going to ask you to back off."

"Back off what?"

"You know," Maitland said.

"Ah, the woman. She's your friend, huh?"

"Yes. She's done nothing to you. She doesn't even know you. Why don't you forget about her."

Wong regarded Maitland for a moment. He said, "If I could, I would. But it's too late for that."

Maitland said, "She's not part of your world. She's nobody to you. Just forget about her. She doesn't know you."

Wong said, "But that doesn't matter. She was in the wrong place at the wrong time. I can't help that."

"Call it off," Maitland said. "She's not in a position to threaten you. Neither am I. We're nobodies, Wong. Forget about us."

Wong said, "I understand you were a policeman."

"I used to be."

"But no more," Wong said. "A disgrace, perhaps?"

"I don't think so," Maitland said. "I wasn't crooked, if that's what you're suggesting."

"Unlike me?" Wong said.

"Yeah. Unlike you."

Hsu-shen raised his hand for another strike. Wong made a gesture to him to hold it and he did.

"Mr. Maitland, we have here a cultural misunderstanding. In China, there is no shame in working for both sides. Indeed, there is no 'side.' In Taiwan and the Mainland, the triads are considered patriotic. In this country, the politicians declare a war on drugs. They deem it necessary to call it a war. For what? To get money through government funding, make their government more powerful. But narcotics is a business, like cigarettes or alcohol or even gambling. It always has been. When it's approached realistically, bloodshed is avoided."

Maitland stared at this man. And in a few moments, he realized that he meant what he was saying.

Maitland said, "Okay. I'm sympathetic to your worldview. You want power and you want to control the heroin market in the Midwest. Fine. Leave us out of it."

Wong was shaking his head again. "I told you, it's too late for that. Tell us where the woman is. You have my word that we'll deal with her humanely. She will not be savaged."

But she'll still be dead, Maitland thought. And again he was struck by how this man was convinced of his own rationality.

Wong said, "Do you know what the triads do? Do you? When a debt has not been paid, we force the man to watch while his wife or daughter is raped and killed before him. And then even after that is done, we still demand that the debt be paid." Wong paused. Then he said, "We will find her sooner or later without your help. But if you don't help, this is what will happen. My point is, you're not helping her with your silence. You're only harming her."

Maitland said nothing.

Hsu-shen said in Cantonese, "Let me work on him."

Wong answered in Cantonese, saying, "No. We have to meet with Cho-jen. Tonight. I'll need you with me. Along with the other bodyguards." Wong glanced at Maitland. He said, "Look, it's working on him already. Let him sit here for a couple of hours and think about what I've said. It's the quickest way to find out where the woman is."

Hsu-shen wanted to torture the American now. But it was a boost to his place in the Wu-Chai to be seated next to Wong when he met with the Red Lantern. Cho-jen had made contact for negotiations sooner than expected. Cho-jen would have his top bodyguards with him too.

Hsu-shen did not speak. He merely gave a bow of his head to show submission.

Wong said in English, "I've an important meeting. Out of respect, I'm going to give you some time to think about what you should do." Wong said something in Cantonese to the other men. Then he left the room.

Wong walked downstairs with Hsu-shen and another bodyguard. When they came out the front door to the porch, the other bodyguards straightened up, and began their move to the vehicles. Wong and Hsu-shen got into the Mercedes with two other men. The remaining four bodyguards climbed into a black Range Rover and followed them down the dirt path. Soon, the farmhouse was out of sight.

A modest two-story wooden house in the middle of an Illinois prairie. A sloping roof over the front porch, the roof tiles faded to beige. The lights coming through the second-floor windows. Quiet and with little noise apart from the crickets and birds and the faint whir of the air conditioner window unit.

■ ■ ■ ■

They had left three men in the room with him. One of them held a short-barreled shotgun, the other two holding handguns. They cast him bored glances but little more. They weren't afraid of him, sitting in a chair with his hands tied behind his back. It was something, Maitland thought. They had not been instructed to torture him. They were just supposed to keep him there until Wong came back.

From his meeting.

With who?

What did it matter? Wong was letting the time work against him. Leaving Maitland alone to think about the consequences of his actions. *Don't tell us where the woman is and it will be bad for you. Worse for her.* Words to that effect and by God, he meant it too.

They could physically torture him and maybe that would be better. Maybe that would be better than leaving him alone with three goons to keep him guard and not much to do but wonder what they would do to her if they did find her . . . when they found her. They would bring her back here and . . .

Something in the window.

Maitland looked out to the darkness. Trees, but they were not close. There was a roof out there, probably hanging over the front porch. The air conditioner window unit thrumming, cooling the room . . .

Something over it. A shadow . . .

Then gone.

Maitland turned his attention away from it. He looked at the man with the shotgun. Gave him a little smile. The man didn't smile back. Maitland looked at the other two men. They didn't look back at him.

A rap.

A bump from the window unit.

Then another.

Like it had been kicked.

The guards in the room looked at one another. Confused, and curious. One of them took his handgun out of his belt and slowly approached the window above the air conditioner. He put his hand on it to see if that would tell him something. It didn't and he looked out the window above.

The window blew apart at the same time the gun fired. The bullet smashed into the man's forehead and he went stumbling back before he hit the ground.

Frank Chang had the muzzle of the gun

pressed almost flush with the glass when he fired and when it was done he knew the man on the other side was dead. He stepped back from the window and moved behind the cover of a brick chimney stack. Counted about one second when the barrage of gunfire came through the windows. The windows being completely blown out and the air-conditioning unit bucking and bending as bullets slammed into it.

And now shotgun blasts were coming out the window on the other side of him. And then it stopped.

Maitland was still in his chair. A captive audience. A dead man lying on the floor only a few feet in front of him. His gun a couple of feet from his dead hand.

The man with the shotgun swung it on Maitland. Still tied to the chair, but coveting that handgun and the man with the shotgun knowing it too.

The man with the shotgun said, "You stay there." Then he kicked the handgun away from Maitland's chair. He said to the other man, "I'm going out front. Stay with him."

He went out the door and the man he left behind pointed his handgun at Maitland's face, like it had been his fault. Maitland knew the man wanted to kill him then, but he had been here when Wong gave his instructions and Maitland was to be kept alive so he could see his woman raped in front of him.

The man with the shotgun, whose name was Eddie Lok, went out the front door onto the porch. He pointed the shotgun up at the ceiling and fired a blast, then two more and then another. He wanted to hear a man cry out, then have the satisfaction of seeing the man roll off the roof and onto the ground.

Nothing.

Frank Chang had climbed off the top of the porch and onto the roof. He was now in a sitting position, almost to the peak of the roof.

Eddie Lok moved out from under the porch roof, his shotgun pointed to the top. Moved out of cover of the porch roof, and then further out until he could see there was no one up there anymore.

Up top, Frank Chang reclined his body, then lay with his back on the roof.

Eddie Lok moved further away from the house.

Frank Chang scooted over the peak of the roof, then began scraping down the other side. He stayed on his belly as he crawled to the east side of the house, cautious, because there was no guard on the edge and if he wasn't careful he would fall off.

Eddie Lok gave up on the front, started moving around to the side, telling himself the man had to be still up there because he hadn't seen him on the porch, hadn't seen him go for the back door.

Frank Chang had to put the gun in his left hand, laying flat now on his stomach. Knowing he couldn't put his head out over the edge because that would expose it and the spread on a shotgun didn't require precise aim, the shot would take half of his face off anyway.

So he lay there and listened. Listened for the man to try to come around the side . . .

Eddie Lok crept on the grass, hating the darkness, but knowing it was here and there was nothing that could be done about it. The only light was from the moon, not quite full, but giving it something, a little light to walk by and the light on the grass changed, an extra shadow and Eddie Lok looked up as the first shot came —

Frank spread out his right arm to keep himself on the roof and he fired the second shot and then two more and he saw the man buck as the bullets tore into his chest and shoulder and the shotgun was pointed straight up as it went off one last time and Eddie Lok fell on his back.

Upstairs, the last man looked at Maitland and again he pointed the gun at him.

Maitland said, "You're not supposed to kill me. They told you that."

"Shut up," the man said. "You brought this."

"I don't know anything about it. It's your gang that's in the war."

"Shut up before I kill you."

"Maybe your friend's okay," Maitland said. "Why don't you go check on him?"

"You shut your fucking mouth."

The man went against the wall, away from the windows. He racked the slide on his handgun. He had done it already, Maitland knew, and was not surprised when a bullet came tumbling out.

Now the man raised the pistol and pointed it at the bedroom door. Waiting for someone to come through it. Aiming for it and he wanted to fire now but he couldn't because he needed to conserve the ammo, aiming and waiting and glancing occasionally back at the windows to see if the vampire would return. Dead man on the floor and he was gone for good, the air conditioner still turning but making a strained, ugly noise because it had been shot to bits . . .

The guard put his eyes back on the door. Fearing, but waiting and anticipating, because if they weren't coming through the windows, they would be coming through the door.

And then the door was kicked open.

The guard raised his arm to fire and it was Eddie Lok in the doorway, a bloody apparition and the guard fired two shots at him anyway because the adrenalin was too much by then and there was a hand sticking out from Eddie Lok's side, as if he had a third, and a gun at the end of it barked out three shots and knocked the guard against the wall, splattering it with the guard's blood.

The guard slumped to the floor.

Frank Chang gave Eddie Lok's body a small push and it fell to the ground. Now there were three dead men in the room.

THIRTY-FOUR

Frank Chang was shaking his head at him. He said, "You should have known better."

Maitland said, "What do you mean?"

"Than to follow that woman into the grocer. You walked into a trap."

"You were following the girl?"

"I was watching the store. You were watching the girl. Why didn't they kill you there?"

"They want something from me."

"What?"

"Listen, I don't like conversing like this. You going to untie me or what?"

Frank Chang came around the back of the chair and loosened the bonds. Then he got the knots untied and Maitland got to his feet. He looked about the room.

Maitland said, "Why didn't you come in sooner?"

Frank Chang said, "There were too many men. I had to wait."

"That makes sense," Maitland said.

"Wong and Hsu-shen left."

"Where?"

"He said he had an important meeting. He said something to them in Chinese, I couldn't understand. Listen, we have to find them. They're going to kill Bianca."

"I already told you that."

"Well, now they've told me that."

Maitland picked up the handgun that had belonged to the man by the air conditioner. It was a .357 revolver with a six-inch barrel. Maitland turned to Chang.

Chang was taking a cell phone out of Eddie Lok's jacket pocket.

Maitland said, "We need to find them."

Frank Chang smiled. He said, "Why?"

Maitland didn't reply.

Frank said, "The car's outside."

Frank drove the Lexus down the dirt road. Maitland had his window down, the cool country air filling the car. He needed it. Three dead men, the smell of blood . . .

Maitland said, "He said he had an important meeting. Do you know what that's about?"

Frank said, "I saw him leave with seven bodyguards, including Hsu-shen. They're not going to the Chinese Chamber of Commerce."

Maitland said, "Yeah?"

"It's probably a meeting with the Red Lantern."

"What? Like a showdown?"

Frank Chang shook his head again. "No," he said, "not a showdown." He said it like it was a kid's term. "A meeting. A negotiation. The goal is to settle this peacefully."

Maitland said, "Settle things peacefully with gangsters, but rape and murder an innocent woman. That's how it works?"

"Yes. That's how it works." Frank Chang said, "I already told you that."

"Sorry I doubted you." Maitland said, "So what is this?"

"Pardon?"

"What made me worth saving? Worth killing three men for?"

Frank Chang cocked his head. Curious. He said, "I may need you."

Maitland said, "You planning to use me as a shield too?"

"You don't trust me?"

"No."

"Such ingratitude," Frank said, "after saving your life."

"You'll get over it," Maitland said. "Presuming they are meeting with the Red Lantern. Where would this be?"

"I don't know."

And Maitland pictured the vast spread that was Chicagoland. Riding with an assassin on a country road, miles from nowhere. Both of them alive but neither one of them knowing where to go.

Frank Chang said, "There wouldn't be much you could do, anyway. Too many men there. Guards for both the Wu-Chai and the Red Lantern." Frank looked at Maitland. "You might stick out," he said. "Sometimes, it's best to wait."

"Not this time," Maitland said.

He wanted to do something, now. They would find out soon that he had escaped and then it would start all over again. They might find Bianca before they found him. Find her and do what they said they would do. He could call the police and tell them what happened. And then they would say, okay, start at the beginning: who is this Chinese guy that saved you? Hours upon hours of interrogation. Suspicion of Maitland collaborating with criminals again. *You know, Preston Wong's a very important man around here, are you sure you know what you're accusing him of? You say you heard him say these things, but what were you doing there in the first place? What about these three dead Chinese guys?*

And so forth.

Frank Chang said, "The Chinese have an expression."

"Yeah?" Maitland said. "What's that?"

"I can't remember it specifically. Something about not fighting the river's current."

"How profound," Maitland said. "Tell me, does it help us here?"

"Maybe," Frank said. He took Eddie Lok's cell phone out of his jacket pocket. He went through the dialed numbers catalogue until he found the one that he remembered.

Then the phone was ringing.

Hsu-shen answered.

Hsu-shen was sitting in the back of the Mercedes with Preston Wong, the city's skyline lights coming into view now.

Hsu-shen said, "What do you want, Eddie?"

"Eddie's dead," Frank said. He left it at that, let Hsu-shen figure out the rest of it.

Hsu-shen looked over at Wong.

Hsu-shen said, "The others too?"

"Yes," Frank said. "The bounty hunter's still alive though."

"Where?"

"He's with me." Frank said, "Put Wong on the phone."

Hsu-shen turned to Wong. He said, "It's Chang. He says he's got Maitland."

Preston Wong's expression said, *what?*

And Hsu-shen said, "He's calling from Eddie's phone."

Wong took Hsu-shen's phone. He said, "Frank? We've been looking for you."

Frank Chang switched to Cantonese. He said, "Have you?"

"Yes. It seems you skipped out."

Frank laughed. "I do that sometimes. When I've been betrayed."

Wong said, "Did we hurt your feelings?"

"Yes," Frank said. "My spirit is wounded. But it will mend."

"How soon will that be?"

"As soon as we negotiate our own settlement."

"How so?"

"Pay me what you owe me. Plus another fifty thousand for the betrayal. In exchange, I'll give you the bounty hunter."

"And then what?"

"And then I'll leave town. You'll remain on peaceful terms with the White Lotus and with the Red Lantern." Frank said, "It's a fair offer, Wong."

Wong said, "How do you know I'm not already on fair terms with the White Lotus? How do you know I wasn't doing them a favor?"

"I'm betting you weren't," Frank said.

"What do you say?"

Wong said, "Maitland is with you?"

Frank Chang was looking at him now. "Yes," he said. "He's my prisoner now."

Wong said, "Kill him yourself then. I'll pay you for it later."

"I've heard that before," Frank said. "Wong, I can bring him to you, or I can drop him off at the police station. It's up to you."

Wong hesitated. He looked over at Hsu-shen, but Hsu-shen wasn't saying anything.

Wong said, "I have an important meeting."

"Postpone it," Frank said. "It will be better for you to have this out of the way."

Wong was looking at Hsu-shen again. He said, "It will take me some time to get that much money."

"How long?"

"An hour. I can meet you in an hour."

Frank said, "Where?"

"There is an abandoned factory in the western part of town. 322 West Gann Street. Can you find it?"

"Yes. 322 West Gann. I'll see you in an hour," Frank said.

THIRTY-FIVE

Frank thought this part of the city was even worse than the south. The victim of not having half a million or so Chinese to clean it up. There was trash and debris in the streets, abandoned cars with their windows smashed out, houses and buildings ravaged by fire, the remaining parts covered with obscenities saying bad things about the police. They passed ruins from a more pleasant past: an eastern orthodox church, its windows knocked out or boarded up, discarded automobile tires piled up in the parking lot; concrete piles and rubble from a convent building that had been razed to the ground; empty homes and businesses. Everywhere signs of arson, bankruptcy, crime, and decay.

Frank said, "Do people live here?"

"Not many," Maitland said. "Vagrants, squatters, but there's no heat or running water. There's no infrastructure."

"Why don't they clear it out?"

"It's cheaper just to leave it here. Money's invested north and further west. This is a ghost town."

There were no other cars to be seen. No cars that were moving. No traffic, no police presence. No signs of a living, breathing community. Empty, dark, and isolated. Wong had thought before choosing this place.

Maitland pointed. "That's it," he said.

They were south of the factory complex. A dilapidated fence coming out of tall grass and weeds and beyond that the gray and faded red brick of the factory buildings. There was a water tower sprouting up from the middle of the complex, running about fifty yards parallel to a seven-story smokestack. On the smokestack, white letters spelled out "Marathon Steel."

Between the fence and the factory there was an old parking lot, potholed and crumbling. It extended about three quarters of a football field.

Maitland said, "They could have a man in that tower with a rifle."

"It's dark," Frank said.

Maitland said, "Doesn't matter. I'm not walking through that open ground."

"Okay," Frank said. "We'll go around the side."

Frank drove around the block and parked the Lexus. They walked to the fence and then along it until they saw a piece of it folded back on itself.

Frank gestured to the hole. "Go ahead," he said.

"No," Maitland said. "After you."

Frank went first through the hole, Maitland after him.

They walked closer to the buildings, and soon they were feeling the complex up close. It was still and dead and unsettling. Were there some noise, it would be something of a comfort. A windmill or a car or an approaching train. Something. But there was no sound. Just the structures looming around them.

Dark, the only light coming from a street lamp about a block away. One of the few lamps left in this area that had not been shot out. A darkness you had to adjust your eyesight to and tell yourself that it was good enough.

When they got closer to the buildings, they could make out railroad tracks leading up to a loading dock. And without speaking to each other, they began to drift apart. Both of them feeling that they would be safer that way, not wanting to offer an easy target for well-grouped shots. And when they were almost at the loading dock they were almost fifteen feet apart and that was when the man stepped out of the doorway, racking the pump on a sawed-off shotgun and pointing and Frank drew and shot the man in the chest.

The man fell off the loading dock and hit the ground.

A Chinese man, wearing a white T-shirt and a red bandanna. He struggled to get up and Frank shot him again.

Chang and Maitland spread further apart.

Maitland kept the loading dock to his left, protecting the lower part of his body as he moved alongside of it, bending over now, so that he would not be seen, keeping his steps quiet and slow, looking at intervals in the dark holes in the building beyond. He moved and kept moving and after several yards, he saw an empty doorway. He climbed onto the dock and went toward it.

Got to the side and did the cop's quick head thrust, out and then back to see if anyone was there.

There wasn't and he stepped inside.

A damp, trashy smell in here. The summer air warming up a stench. Maitland kept his back to the wall, made himself stay still for a few moments as he waited for his eyesight to readjust to an even darker place.

There *was* light. Little of it, creeping through the empty holes that had once been windows. Light was coming, refining itself to a maximum point, and Maitland waited for it, while he kept his mouth shut and breathed through his nose.

He did not count seconds or let himself wonder how long he waited there. But soon he became aware of another's presence. A man stirring, breathing. His feet shuffling on wet ground.

Maitland looked to his left. Looked for squares and angles and let them come into form and soon he could see the thing that was not square and angled. The form of a man.

Holding a rifle. Looking out the window for him.

Maitland kept his back to the wall. He scooted five feet, and then ten. Then twenty.

Any closer and the man would hear him.

Maitland raised the .357 revolver and clicked the hammer back.

Then said, "Put it down."

The man swung on him, leveling the rifle to fire, and Maitland pulled his trigger and shot the man in the chest, the shot echoing off the inside walls.

I told you, Maitland thought. But still feeling glad that the other was dead and he was alive and that was when he heard the quasi-mechanical sound of a switch being thrown and then there was harsh, open light flooding down from above.

Light. Not on him directly, but he was illuminated now. A fucking spotlight, battery operated, but with one million candlepower and the guys that were behind it were above him like prison guards in a tower and he was the fugitive out in the open.

There. Up there on a balcony that was next to an old floor supervisor's office and Maitland ran for the window as machine gun fire started coming down from the balcony. The shots wild at first, but getting more disciplined as Maitland got to the window and jumped out headfirst.

Maitland ran away from the window, kept going away from it, hoping there weren't any more men waiting out by the dock.

Frank heard the distinct sound of the .357 revolver. A pause and then the sound of machine gun fire. He was still on the outside of the factory building. Out in the open, but it was dark where he was. He kept his back flush against the wall. There was a doorway to his right, the door long since gone. He saw light emit from the door. Then heard footsteps.

Frank straightened up, tried to put himself into the wall.

A man came out of the doorway, a pistol at his side.

Frank said, "Hey."

The man turned, his chest now exposed. Raised his arm to point his gun and Frank shot him.

Wong stood on the balcony alongside Hsu-shen and two other men. One of the men was holding the spotlight, sweeping it back and forth. The other was the one holding the machine gun.

They heard the last gunshot.

Wong turned to Hsu-shen, a questioning look in his expression.

Hsu-shen said, "A different sound."

"Chang," Wong said.

Hsu-shen said, "He deceived us."

Wong grunted. Well, yes. Three of their men killed and counting himself there were now five left. They had not heard anything from their man in the water tower. That one had a high-powered rifle with an infrared scope, but he didn't seem to be doing them any good now.

Wong said to Hsu-shen, "Go after Mait-

land. Take Kwong with you. I'll take Li."
Wong said, "Unless you want Chang."

"No," Hsu-shen said, remembering the
man who had made him scurry from his car
on Highway 41. "I'll take the *gwai-lo.*"

The man in the water tower was short and
stocky and his name was Chew Fat-hei. He
had a Mauser bolt action rifle with an
infrared scope. He had been laying flat on
top of the water tower keeping an eye out
over the vast open parking lot to the east.
But when he heard the first shot, it came
from the north. From the other side of the
factory, out of his view.

Damn.

Another shot following, a pause, and then
machine gun fire.

Coming from inside. Echoing.

Be patient, Chew thought. You can start
climbing down, but then you'll be exposed
to a man on the ground. The rifle would be
slung over his shoulder and he wouldn't be
able to use it while he was holding onto a
ladder. He would be vulnerable. Patience.
They'll come to you.

And that was when he heard another shot.
Not machine gun fire, but from a handgun.

Chew put his head out over the side of
the surface. He put his eye to the scope,

moved it to where the sound had been. Red ground, red and black, and . . . there it was.

It was Angi. His body lying on the ground where he'd been shot.

Chew moved the scope about, fishing, and something darker came into view. There. Against the wall.

Chang.

The assassin from New York. They had told him that Chang was supposed to bring the *gwai-lo* in exchange for money. They had told him to kill Chang when he saw him, that it was okay because the man was a traitor, had betrayed his brothers in New York and in Chicago. That he had shown disrespect to Wong and the Wu-Chai. They told Chew these things as if he needed to hear them. He didn't.

Chew looked down on the assassin, made mental adjustments for trajectory and windage, put the crosshairs on the man's chest, and squeezed the trigger.

After the shot, Chew took his eye off the scope and looked down.

Shit. The man was not on his back, not sucking in air with a heavy chest wound. He must have moved before the trigger had been squeezed.

Frank Chang *had* moved. He had started to

move forward, his plan to jump past the door and go around the other side of the factory. And as he stepped the shot came from above and zipped through a space about four inches above his left breast. It went out the back, through his left shoulder blade. He ran forward, kept running, and then he was under the water tower.

The water tower tank sat atop three support arms at the circumference and a thick pipe going up the center. The water pipe. Shit. Maitland had warned him about the water tower. The American having more cowboy in him than Chang.

Frank looked up the pipe. Then he looked at the three support arms. One of them had a ladder attached to the side that would take you to the top.

Frank was wheezing now, wondering if the bullet had punctured his lung. He could climb up the ladder and maybe surprise the rifleman up top. But he doubted he would make it. Even if the rifle were out of shots, Frank would probably fall on his own halfway up.

Or maybe the shooter would try to come down the ladder and Frank would be able to pick him off then.

Unlikely.

The water tower was between two buildings. The distance from the water tower to the first building was about thirty yards. The distance to the second building was between ten and twenty. A short run and then he would be under the cover of an overhang. If he made that, he could get inside the second building and find some way to get on top of it. Maybe get a clearer shot at the rifleman.

Yeah, Frank thought. With a handgun. Shooting up five or six stories in the dark.

Frank looked up. The water tank forming a dark bulb above. Frank estimated the diameter was about twelve feet across. The man would not be able to cover all sides at once. If there was only one man. If he were still watching the other side, Frank could run this side and cross the distance before the other was aware. And there was more than one side.

Frank ran to the cover of the second building.

The water tower shooter was ready for it. Lying on his stomach waiting with his finger on the trigger.

But it's not easy to hit a running target in the dark. Not when you're looking down on it. Two shots *thwacked* into the ground, but both of them missed Frank Chang and then he was under the cover of the second building's overhang.

And now Chew was on his feet, leaning out over the precipice, his rifle pointing down, and that was when Frank Chang stepped out and pointed his gun and shot up at the shadow standing on the edge.

His shots did not connect. It was too far up and a handgun's accuracy isn't much past thirty yards even in broad daylight. His first shot hit the bottom of the water tank, his second hit the side and came out top somewhere near the center, but the third came up and pierced through the side and out the top and hit Chew in the lower leg.

It missed bone, but Chew cried out in pain and jumped involuntarily as if he'd been bitten by a snake. Hopping on one leg, he lost his balance on the edge and his yelp of pain became a scream as he went out into free space and he seemed to hang in the air for a second before he began to plummet and see the ground hurtling up toward him.

Frank could not see him land from where he was. But he heard the sickening *whump*. He peered around the corner and saw the broken heap lying about twenty yards away.

Maitland got to the side of the building, heard a gunshot and then rifle fire. He could go around the other side of the building, but that was where the men with machine guns were. He saw trees and brush up ahead, a house on the other side, and he ran for the trees.

He heard voices then, small shouts in Chinese, and then there was gunfire and Maitland got to the trees and dropped to his belly. No sound then, no voices. But he knew they had seen him and they were debating now about coming in after him. There were trees around him, little more than dirty brush and some foliage. It was not the cover of a forest and he would be a fool to think it was. He saw a field and a telephone pole beyond. On the other side of the field was a burned-out house.

Maitland lay on his stomach and looked toward the factory.

Two men approaching. One of them holding the machine gun, the other a pistol at his side. Maybe. It was dark and there was brush in between. Maitland still had the .357 revolver. It had a long six-inch barrel, but it was dark and the hunters were too far away. He could fire at them, set off a flash among the trees, and the machine gun would give his cover a good raking and that would be the end of him.

Lying on his stomach in wet grass, Maitland thought about it.

He could crawl and then run out the other

side of the trees. Then the trees would be between him and his pursuers and maybe he could make it to the abandoned house. He could hold the house, use it as cover, and maybe pick them off if they came close.

It was too dark out here. Too dark among the trees. If they had a flashlight, they could beam it across the trees, pick out a white man in clothes contrasting with the nature and open up.

They were moving closer now. Closer to the trees. Spreading out and now Maitland could see that the second man was Hsu-shen. The one he had taken a shot at on Highway 41. He had missed that day and now he was really sorry about it. He should have put him down then, but he hadn't and now he was on his belly in damp ground waiting for them to find him and kill him. He could aim and hit Hsu-shen now. Maybe. But if he missed, the machine gunner would open up on him and probably connect. Even if he didn't miss, the machine gunner would do that.

Let them come closer, he thought. Closer and he would be able to get a shot. Get a shot that wouldn't be a risk. Don't gamble, he thought. Not now.

And now they were close enough that he could practically hear them breathing, and

Maitland knew that he wouldn't be able to do it while lying down. There would be too much in the way, too much between him and them. He would have to stand up, point and shoot and connect, and put the machine gunner down. Do that and swing left and do the same to Hsu-shen.

And now they were close enough that he felt he had to do it. Do it now, before they get too close and see you first.

Maitland stood.

The machine gunner turned his head at the sound and Maitland fired three times, the shots cracking out in the night and he saw the machine gunner flip back in the air as if he had run into an unseen clothesline. The man up and then on his back and hopefully that was the end of him.

One bullet left in the revolver and Maitland turned to fire on Hsu-shen.

But Hsu-shen was gone.

Maitland whirled to his right. Looking for the man, hoping that he had run away, back to the factory, but knowing somewhere that the man had come into the trees as well. Knowing he was not going to leave him alone this time. He could feel him nearby.

Maitland heard the crash of brush. Someone coming through. Maitland turned and pointed the weapon, saw a form, and fired.

Then cursed himself. It was his last bullet. Holding a useless revolver in his hand now. A four-pound piece of steel, not making him feel any more virile at this moment. Maybe Hsu-shen didn't know he was out. Didn't know he was carrying a revolver. If he did know, he would be laughing his ass off, waiting for Maitland to come out of the trees, hat in hand.

Maitland turned and saw the light increase. The field. Maitland crouched. Waited.

He let a minute pass. Or what he thought was a minute. It could have been longer or shorter, he didn't know. But he wanted to hear something, hear the presence of the hunter coming after him. Wanted to hear where the other was. Wanted to know.

After a time, he heard movement. Heard steps.

And then he saw it. The silhouette of a man, near the back of the trees, against the field. Hsu-shen had gone all the way around and he hadn't known it. Smart, Maitland thought. And then he sprang, crashing through the brush and Hsu-shen turned toward the trees, fired in the darkness, missing and Maitland came out and tackled him.

They both went to the ground. Maitland

landing on top of him and they both grunted and Maitland could see that the impact had knocked the gun loose from Hsu-shen, but where was the gun? Looking for it on the ground in the dark and that was when Hsu-shen made his first strike. A palm lightning out to Maitland's temple, but missing and hitting him on the cheek. It was enough to knock Maitland on his ass and then Hsu-shen was on his feet and Maitland had to scramble back to get distance before he could stand up himself.

Maitland looked at Hsu-shen then and thought, *Oh, shit. Martial arts.*

Hsu-shen standing in a sideways position, his head tilted forward, his eyes intent, legs in the horse stance. Hsu-shen's left hand was extended and his fingers were in a sort of dragon claw, his right hand in a fist chambered back behind his head. And Maitland thought, he's going to beat me to death. This is how he wants it. Would that it were only a pose.

Hsu-shen sprang forward and his left hand flashed to Maitland's neck. It missed the death spot, but then Hsu-shen used the same hand to deliver a knife shot into Maitland's ribs and you could hear that one and Maitland felt his breath leave him, but he managed to bring a fist down onto the man's shoulder, which availed him nothing as Hsu-shen brought a sharp kick up into Maitland's solar plexus and the breath left him again and this time he went down.

He was on his back when he saw Hsu-shen spring above him and he rolled before Hsu-shen could come down and spear a foot into his neck and then he was up and he wanted to run but Hsu-shen would probably catch him and then kill him and he would be out of breath then, so he stepped back as Hsu-shen feinted then rushed him but Maitland stepped into it and they smacked into each other. Maitland grabbed one of Hsu-shen's wrists with one hand and the back of his shirt with the other, holding him in that moment, and Maitland snapped his head into Hsu-shen's face.

Hsu-shen grunted and Maitland could hear his nose crack, but Hsu-shen still had a free hand and he used it to drive a hard punch into Maitland's kidneys and Maitland couldn't help but relax his grip on the man and Hsu-shen punched Maitland in the face and drove him back.

They squared off again. Hsu-shen's nose bleeding and broken, but Maitland took little comfort in that. Typical guy in a bar will stop fighting if his nose is broken. But a combat fighter just . . . doesn't . . . care. They keep going until the other man is dead.

Hsu-shen was hovering before him, like a cobra, and then the cobra struck. A hand flashing out to Maitland's eyes, temporarily blinding him, and he couldn't help but close them and there followed two more punches to his face and then a strong kick to his midsection. Maitland went down again.

Maitland was on his back, reaching into his front pants pocket, and then Hsu-shen was on top of him, grabbing his shirt front to hold him steady for a strike that would have driven Maitland's nose up into his cerebral cortex and Maitland pulled the car keys out of his pocket and placed the longest one between his fingers and swung it in an arc across Hsu-shen's eyes.

He heard Hsu-shen cry out as he felt contact, the top of the key missing the eyes but cutting into Hsu-shen's already broken, bloody nose and Hsu-shen fell back and Maitland got off the ground as Hsu-shen rose from his sitting position to his knees and Maitland was running now and Hsu-shen got up and went after him but didn't put it together until Maitland dropped to his knees and picked up Hsu-shen's gun and turned and fired once and then again as Hsu-shen leaped in the air and fell on him.

THIRTY-SIX

Frank Chang's head and chest were hurting. He could feel the wound on his back, see some of it on his front. He was conscious of the dampness and the stain of blood on his jacket. He felt a little drunk. He remembered an old man once telling him that the senses were actually more attuned when he was intoxicated. Frank had not believed him then. Nor now. Old men could be fools too. Old fools.

After the man had dropped off the tower, Frank had not gone into the second building. He had remained under the overhang. It was a smaller loading dock, just enough for a small truck to back up to and be kept out of the rain.

All the entrances at this dock were boarded up. Frank knew he did not have the strength to pull down the board. Did not have the strength to do much more than stay here and wait for them to come to him.

He checked his weapon. His .45 automatic, the rounds courtesy of the bounty hunter. He preferred it to the Browning nine-millimeter.

He was stuck in this corner. They might come for him from the front, if they were stupid or if they were unaware of him. That would be nice. But not probable. They would come from the corners, along the walls. Maybe one of them would distract him, while the others came around the other corner and finished him. Turned out his light and he would never see Mott Street again. His service to the White Lotus complete.

He had joined them, become one of them, and had never really looked back. Could he honestly say that he had no choice? That it was either the life of a triad member or one of indignity? The gun and violence and threats or washing dishes in a tiny kitchen in Chinatown. Ah. Would it have been so limited? He had had other options. He should have looked into them.

But he knew he probably wouldn't have. This was the life he had wanted. And he had known that it would involve dealing with the Preston Wongs of this world. He had not kidded himself on that score. It was what he had chosen.

A noise. Someone approaching.

Coming from his right . . .

Frank Chang scooted himself to the corner of the dock. Got himself to the corner of the platform and put himself back into the wall. He raised his .45 against the wall, level with his shoulder.

A man came to the corner, a gun at his side, and Frank placed the muzzle of the .45 against his temple.

Frank said, "Which one are you?"

He could not have been much more than seventeen. Older than Frank had been when he got pulled into this business. But still a boy.

The boy said, "Li."

"Drop that gun, Li."

Li let it clatter to the ground.

Frank pressed the gun further to the boy's head. Frank said, "Run away."

The kid took off. Frank watched him cross the parking lot, between the weeds, and then he was gone.

He moved back to the center of the loading dock corner. His gun was at his side and he felt a wave of nausea, his head swimming, and he put his back against the wall and let himself slide down into a sitting position. He loosened his grip from the gun and let it rest on the ground next to him.

Then he smiled.

Preston Wong was standing in front of him, pointing a handgun.

Wong said, "You've gone soft, Frank."

Frank Chang said, "Maybe he'll join the Peace Corps. Or become a priest."

Wong was smiling now, shaking his head. "Frank," he said. "You should have left town when you had the chance. Why didn't you?"

Frank said, "You owed me money." It was face, after all. Perhaps the only thing he had maintained a belief in.

Wong understood this, but said, "There would have been no shame in surviving." Wong raised his arm to fire.

Wong's finger was on the trigger when the shot came from his right. The first one catching him in his rib cage, then a second shot going in after it.

Wong fell to his side, the life coming out of him. He lived long enough to look over to his right and see Maitland standing nearby, the gun still in his hand. It was the last thing he saw.

Maitland walked over to him. Crouched down to feel for a pulse. There wasn't one and Maitland felt a cold satisfaction in it. He hoisted himself up onto the loading dock and walked over to the assassin.

Frank looked at the marks on Maitland's face. "You've been fighting," he said.

"Yeah," Maitland said. He was still holding Hsu-shen's gun. He saw the shattered upper body of Chang and said, "Jesus."

"You were right," Frank said. "There was a man on the tower. He had a rifle."

"Oh, Jesus," Maitland said. "We have to get you to a hospital."

Frank shook his head. He could no longer feel sensation in his finger tips. The pain in his chest and head had subsided, but he knew that was only because his nervous system was slowly shutting down. His legs were cold and numb from the loss of blood. He had a few minutes at best.

Frank said, "It's no use. Too much blood." Frank smiled. "I guess you thought you were saving my life."

"Yeah," Maitland said. "I thought."

Frank Chang said, "Don't worry about it. Just sit with me for a minute, will you?"

"Okay," Maitland said.

THIRTY-SEVEN

He brought Bianca home the next morning.

When she first saw him, her attention was drawn to the bruises and cuts on his face. She put her fingers on his cheek and said, "What happened?"

"I'd rather not talk about it," he said. "It's over, though."

"It's safe now?"

"Yeah. It's safe."

But driving back he told her that Frank Chang was dead. He told her that that was the man's name. He told her that the man's name was one of the last things he had found out about him.

Bianca said, "You didn't . . . ?" Somehow, she didn't want the man's killer to have been Evan.

"No," Maitland said. "It wasn't me. He saved my life, in fact. Yours too, I guess."

Bianca said, "I didn't even know him. Why would he do that?"

"I don't know, really. I'm not sure it had much to do with us. He never really said."

They drove in silence for a few moments. Bianca looked out the window, the Wisconsin state line behind them now and the traffic began to thicken as they approached the outskirts of greater Chicago.

Bianca said, "The summer's coming to an end, isn't it?"

She was looking away from him. If she was crying, he couldn't tell. Maitland put his hand on her back, let it rest there for a moment before he put it back on the steering wheel.

When he got back to his apartment a couple of hours later, Julie was washing dishes in his kitchen sink. He stood at the back door, watching her, and he felt a stab of pain. A domestic scene with her, one he suspected he would not see again.

She turned around and regarded him quietly before saying anything.

Maitland said, "Hey."

"Hey." She was studying the bruises on his face as well.

Maitland said, "I'm okay."

Julie said, "I was just cleaning a few things up before I . . . well, you know."

"I know," Maitland said. He looked at a

suitcase on the floor, resting by the recliner chair. It was packed.

She was studying him again, reading his expression and his wounds. She seemed to give an inward sigh and then she said, "If I were on duty, I'd ask where you were last night."

"Are you on duty?"

"No."

He found he could not look at her when he said, "I'm sorry, Julie."

"I'm sorry, too." She said, "I could have helped you, you know."

Maitland wasn't sure she could have. He had made a conscious decision to leave her out of it. He had told himself it was for her good too. He was too tired now to think about whether or not he believed it. He didn't answer her now.

Julie picked up her suitcase.

And Maitland said, "You need help?" Feeling lame as soon as he said it.

She shook her head and drifted over to him. Their shoulders brushed up against each other as they stood side to side, facing opposite directions, neither one quite making eye contact with the other. She didn't kiss him on the cheek or take his hand. But for a moment she put her face against his shoulder. Then she moved to the back door as she said, "Goodbye, Evan."

"Goodbye, Julie," he said, without turning. Then he heard the back door close and he was alone.

ABOUT THE AUTHOR

James Patrick Hunt was born in Surrey, England, in 1964. He is the author of *Maitland, Maitland Under Siege, Before They Make You Run, The Betrayers, Goodbye Sister Disco,* and *The Assailant.* He resides in Tulsa, Oklahoma.